Professor Cassell's Daughter

By Margaret Bacon

CHAPTER ONE

"Ruth, this is Elizabeth," her father had said, and she had known immediately. She had known not only that he was in love with this Elizabeth and would one day marry her, but also that he assumed that the two of them would be good friends. To be fair to him, it was a justifiable hope; Elizabeth was intelligent, kind and friendly.

But she couldn't be fair to him; fairness is for strangers. He should have known, – he *must* have known – that he was destroying her world, everything they had built up together over the years, just the two of them. People who have been as close as she and her father had been all her life know such things without words.

It was nobody's fault; it was the way life had shaped them. She had only been a few months old when her mother was taken ill. For five years her father had somehow cared for his sick wife, looked after their tiny daughter and made a success of his job at the university. For as long as she could remember, people had said he was marvellous. It was amazing, domestic helps would say as they peeled vegetables to be left in pans of water and put out notes for tradesmen, amazing how he managed. Good as a woman, he was.

She sensed his grief when her mother died although she did not share it. He had always been both father and mother to her. She didn't miss her mother; years later when she heard her school friends grumbling about their mothers, she was quite glad that she had been bereaved. Only as she grew older did she understand that his deprivation had been greater than hers. She told him that she wouldn't mind if he remarried. And she believed it; filial love is without jealousy or possessiveness.

But he had always shaken his head. He'd had had one perfect marriage, he said, and that should be enough for any man. The hardest thing he had to bear after his wife had died, he told Ruth years later, was the way people had said to him, "You're still young; plenty of time to start life again when the right woman comes along." Even if they didn't say it in so many words, they implied it; while condoling with him on the loss of the best and bravest of wives, they would suggest that it would not be impossible to replace her.

She was fifteen when they moved from the provincial university town to London just after the war. She was shocked to see bomb sites and streets of derelict houses, as they walked from estate agent to estate agent, all of whom talked gloomily about hundreds of people coming back to London now the war was over and of the shortage of houses, most of them damaged and neglected. The only house they could find that was near both to his work and her school was, as the estate agent said, "Ripe for improvement."

"Then we'll improve it together, you and I," he told her, as they looked around the shabby rooms.

Together they haunted hardware shops and joiners' yards in search of scarce materials, together they measured and fitted, sawed and hammered and finally decorated. Together they made a home.

It was a slow business; he was not a practical man; tall, donnish and bespectacled, he did everything with great deliberation, having spent hours scowling over drawings and DIY manuals.

"I'm starting on your bedroom tomorrow," he told her on the day she left school.

"Why? We've done it, it's all right."

"I'm going to make it more than all right. It was all right for a schoolgirl, but not for a university student. It's going to have fitted everything, boxed in basin, concealed lighting. And a thick white carpet instead of that threadbare old haircoard. It will be not so much a bedroom, more boudoir."

She laughed.

"It sounds very glamorous. I hope it won't outclass me."

"Nothing could," he said.

She was in her third year at London University by the time everything was finished to his satisfaction.

"It's exactly as you said it would be," she told him as she stood in her bedroom, digging her toes into the thick white carpet.

"You don't regret not living out in lodgings like the other students?"

"No, I told you at the time, there was no point in going into some grotty digs when I could be here with you. I was just as much part of the student scene as any other of the others, it really made no difference. Except that I came back to our lovely home at night. I probably got more work done too."

"From now on until Finals are over, you're let off all domestic chores. The kitchen's a no-go area. You just concentrate on your work. That's an order."

She laughed and hugged him and in the weeks that followed he allowed nothing to distract her from revision.

"The trouble is," she told him a few weeks later as they celebrated the end of Finals at a restaurant, "that I'll have nothing to blame if I fail."

"Idiot, don't talk like that," he told her, filling up her glass.

"Oh, by the way, they've asked us if anyone was interested in doing a teachers' training course after we've finished at the university. I said I might be."

"But do you want to teach?"

"Not particularly, no."

"Then don't, you goose."

She sighed. She wasn't sure really. Teaching would be very convenient; it would give her roughly the same hours and holidays as his.

"I'll think about it," she said. "Or there might be something connected with the university, I suppose."

"I'll make enquiries," he promised. "But you frighten me sometimes, Ruth. You do have a way of rushing into things. For goodness' sake don't do anything impetuous. It's a big decision, darling."

"Don't worry about that," she told him airily. "I shall explore all possibilities, as they say, before I decide about the course."

True to her word, she bought *The Times Educational Supplement* the next week. There seemed to be only two history posts on offer at the moment: one quite impossible in a boarding school in a remote part of Cornwall, the other ideally suitable in West London. That settled it: she would take the course and hope that there might be a similar job in London available this time next year.

In fact she still had a copy of *The Times Educational Supplement* in her hand, having perused it again on the tube, when she reached the Senate House for the reception given by the History Department. She had arranged to meet her father there, but there was a crowd and at first she couldn't see him. Then she caught sight of him and he came towards her, bringing somebody with him.

"Ruth, this is Elizabeth," he said.

CHAPTER TWO

She sat alone in her compartment on the west-bound train. Her father had been horrified, almost unable to believe that she had accepted this job in Cornwall after a brief interview with the Headmistress who was in London. She hadn't even seen the place, he said. If she must go off and board, let it at least be to a reputable public school, not some dubious establishment that didn't even require a post-graduate teaching qualification. Above all, there was no reason for her to go away; Elizabeth and he both wanted her to live with them.

She wouldn't listen; she wanted it settled quickly. If she waited, there would be discussions, delays, attempts to make her change her mind. Besides it was no good; she couldn't talk to him any more. It wasn't simply that she couldn't share him. Or perhaps it was. She didn't understand it; she was as shocked as he was by her own reaction. It wasn't through lack of trying; she had tried to be sensible, to adjust to the new situation. But she couldn't. It was as if she had for so long been identified as Professor Cassell's daughter, at school, at college, by his colleagues at the university, that she had no other identity. She had seen her life ahead as his daughter, teaching during the day, working alongside him at night. They had often sat so: he at his desk, she at the table by the fire. They didn't disturb each other. They'd gone together to his various functions at the university, herself welcomed as Cassell's daughter, Cassell's daughter. The train seemed to take up the rhythm. But she was no longer Cassell's daughter. She was bereft by his marrying as she had not been by her mother's dying.

In her panic she had cut herself off from her friends too, even from Alastair who had wanted to marry her. She had never taken him seriously, of course, but still he was a good friend. They were part of the old order, these friends, and she seemed to have no choice but to sever all links with the past.

They had all tried to persuade her not to do this. She didn't particularly like children, they pointed out. It was true; she had always got on better with older people. And she was a town-dweller, positively disliked the countryside and yet she was going to live in a remote spot away from theatres, university, libraries, shops. From choice too; that was the irony of it. Don't act impetuously, her father had said. Well, if he didn't want her to act impetuously, he shouldn't have – never mind, never mind…

The train suddenly shot through a tunnel and out on to the very edge of the sea. For miles it ran in and out of chunks of pink rock, with cliffs on one side and waves on the other. Her pleasure in it was so great that she momentarily forgot her dislike of the countryside. But then the sea is different, she reflected, and seeing nature through glass is different; it sets it at a distance, turns it into a scene. It is quite different from having the depressing green stuff all around you. Just as children seen through a window, at play in the garden, have an idyllic quality which they altogether lack at close quarters.

All the same, her mood changed. For the first time she felt a quiver of excitement at the prospect of going among strangers, who neither knew nor cared who she was and what she had been planning to do with her life. It was more than just an escape from the past; it was an entirely fresh start. She would welcome it. Since nobody knew her, she could invent a whole new character for herself, decide what part to play. The possibilities, as she gazed across the sea, seemed endless.

Even when the line turned inland, the new excitement remained with her. She stood up restlessly in the empty compartment and combed her long fair hair in the glass, peering at her face with round blue eyes, rather startled–looking because she was short-sighted. She had been going to get contact lenses but couldn't afford them now. She had refused her father's offer and he had been afraid to insist.

She took her spectacles out of her bag and put them on. The outline of things immediately jumped into prominence. Blurred edges sharpened into clarity. Her own face with its bright pink cheeks which were really more suitable for a country girl. Well, she was quite a cheerful sort of person. She'd never had any reason for being anything else. Her father had done all the worrying on her behalf. She would not think on such lines, she told herself, turning away from her image in the glass.

From Plymouth onwards the train emptied, until she seemed to have it to herself. It meandered through valleys, stopping at little junctions, not seeming eager to arrive. The countryside, now masked by a fine drizzle, was wild and empty. She had never seen anything like it. She and her father had always lived in big cities and even their holidays had been urban; any rural area they ventured into was at least decently populated.

The drizzle changed to heavy rain when she got out at Truro. As she walked along the platform the wind drove against her, blowing her coat open. She shivered as she stood outside waiting for a taxi.

The taxi drive was longer than she'd expected; they were soon out of the town and driving along narrow roads between thick hedges. Occasionally the driver said things she couldn't understand. She murmured polite responses which she hoped were not too inappropriate.

At last they turned up a steep drive which wound its way through an immense and overgrown shrubbery. She wondered if perhaps one of the reasons Mrs Bland, the Headmistress, interviewed applicants in London was to prevent them from knowing quite how remote her educational establishment was. Not that it would have influenced her against it, of course; the remoter the better, as far as she was concerned.

Although it was only six o'clock, the September sky was almost dark as they emerged from the trees; she could scarcely make out the outlines of an old mansion, turreted and pinnacled. There were only two small points of light visible in the whole building as the car pulled up on the gravel outside the massive front door. She paid the man and then – suddenly fearful of being left stranded up here alone – asked him to wait until somebody answered the door. Evidently he didn't understand her any more than she understood him, for he nodded and drove away before she had even rung the bell.

The electric bell having failed to attract attention, she pulled hard on the long iron handle that hung down by the door. There was a loud clattering sound in the distance and then another as the bell-pull came away from its metal framework and she found herself standing clutching it when Mrs Bland appeared at the door.

"Ah, Miss Cassell, do come in," she said, relieving Ruth of the bell pull. "I hope you had a pleasant journey?"

The hall was a vast, cold arena made chiefly of granite, at the end of which heavy swing doors led into a corridor which they crossed into the Headmistress's study. Once through another set of swing doors everything was pleasanter and warmer. The study had a thick carpet, comfortable chairs and a big fire.

"You must be frozen," Mrs Bland said. "Do sit by the fire and I'll ask for tea."

She walked to the far end of the room, opened a cupboard door into what was evidently a service lift and called down a speaking tube a request for tea.

"Antiquated, but it works," she said, returning to the fireside.

She was more relaxed than she had been at their interview in London; this is where she belongs, Ruth thought. A woman of about forty, her hair dark except for a grey streak at the front, she was thickset, but moved with a kind of ponderous grace.

"It's a pity," she said, "that you couldn't have had a chat with your predecessor, Miss Crewe. She was a marvellous person and I was very sorry to lose her. But she had the chance of a job nearer her home, so I couldn't stand in her way."

They talked about the syllabus; although she had been appointed to teach history, Ruth was surprised to find that she was also expected to teach current affairs and a subject call Civics.

"Local government – drains and so on," Mrs Bland said casually. "The parents like their girls to be well informed."

They were interrupted by a knock at the door, which was opened before Mrs Bland had time to respond. A tall willowy woman in her mid-thirties came in carrying a small tray with a silver teapot and hot water jug. She stood holding the tray and looking at Ruth with an uncompromising stare that gave away nothing. She had deep set eyes of a remarkable lavender colour and was disconcertingly beautiful.

"Ah, Esther," Mrs Bland said. "How kind. Miss Cassell, this is our housekeeper, Miss Fairbairn."

Esther Fairbairn put down the tray on a small table and shook hands, but neither spoke nor smiled. Ruth murmured a greeting. Mrs Bland watched them both.

The silence was broken by a creaking and rattling from the far end of the room. Miss Fairbairn walked across to the hatch and opened the doors. After further straining of the ropes the rest of the tea appeared on a big, wooden-sided butler's tray.

It was a substantial tea. She expected the housekeeper to leave them after she had arranged the plates and cups and saucers. But she did not; she settled herself by the fire and even when they had finished eating and Mrs Bland returned to the discussion of Ruth's timetable and the history syllabus, Esther Fairbairn continued to sit there, listening. She didn't speak or even appear interested, but Ruth found her presence unnerving. Mrs Bland seemed to take for granted her right to be there.

"Well, I think we have covered everything," she said at last. "I'm sure you must want to go to your room and unpack. Miss Fairbairn will show you the way."

At the door she paused and said with some embarrassment, "I suppose there won't be any staff supper tonight, will there, Esther?"

"Not until tomorrow when everyone is back."

"Please don't worry about me," Ruth put in. "I shan't want anything else tonight. I shall go to bed early."

"Well, if you're quite sure," Mrs Bland said, with evident relief. "I was going to suggest you join Miss Fairbairn and myself for dinner here, but I quite understand. So wise to have an early night. I hope you sleep well."

She was dismissed. She left the warmth of the study, the friendly presence of Mrs Bland, and followed Esther Fairbairn across the cavernous hall and into the main school corridor. "Your room is on the top floor," Miss Fairbairn remarked as they crossed the stairs. "That is the dining room," she added, nodding towards glass doors through which rows of tables could be dimly discerned. "You will have breakfast there."

Her voice was low and clear and managed to convey a total lack of interest in Ruth's welfare.

It was a wide staircase, gracefully turned. The stone steps were shallow. They climbed together, side-by-side, without speaking.

At the top, Esther Fairbairn paused and said, "On the first floor are the house rooms. In the centre, through the swing doors, are the Headmistress's rooms, above her study. You will, of course, have no reason to go through the swing doors. They are her *private* apartments."

She didn't seem to expect a reply, so Ruth followed her in silence up the next staircase, identical to the first. "On this floor are the girls' dormitories," Miss Fairbairn told her in the bored tones of a guide who is paid to impart information but has no interest whatsoever in how it is received. "The house mistresses' rooms are on this floor."

The third flight of stairs was much narrower and steeper, as if it had once led to the servants' quarters. They climbed more slowly, Ruth following behind. Miss Fairbairn waited at the top, looking down into the deep well of the stairs. Ruth joined her; she could make out the tiny squares of the stone floor in the hall far below. For a moment she had a sickening lurch of dread at the thought of falling over the railings and smashing on to the stone slabs. She saw that Miss Fairbairn was watching her with a faint light of amusement in her deep-set eyes.

"It's a long drop, Miss Cassell," was all she said.

The top corridor was narrow and ill-lit. Her heels clacked on the bare boards. Miss Fairbairn moved silently, evidently soft-shod.

She stopped outside a door, took out a key and unlocked it.

Looking at the room, Ruth wondered why they bothered to lock it; it wasn't as if there was anything worth stealing. It was a big attic room, with a small dormer window, the floor covered in green linoleum and in the corner a high bed shrouded in a mauve counterpane. There was a large wardrobe, a table and a small bookcase. That was all. There was neither rug nor lamp nor anything to soften the harshness of this bare room, which was lit by a single bulb which hung unshaded from the centre of the ceiling.

She saw with relief that there was a gas fire and gas ring.

"I see that your predecessor left you some coffee and sugar," Miss Fairbairn remarked, looking at two jars on the mantelpiece. "You'll be able to make yourself a drink," she added indifferently, ignoring the lack of a kettle, pan or milk.

"Miss Crewe had this room?" Ruth asked.

"Yes, she left last term. Couldn't keep order, you know, so the girls gave her – a bad time."

She smiled as if at some pleasant memory, and left.

After she'd gone, Ruth walked around the room, determined not to be dismayed by it. She would get lamps and a rug when she got her first cheque, she decided as she began to unpack.

The wardrobe somehow contrived to be much smaller inside than out and only had a length of string, suspended between two hooks, on which to hang the coat hangers. The chest of drawers was perforated with woodworm and its drawers, deep and heavy, were difficult to shift. Her few clothes were lost in their cavernous depths.

Having quickly unpacked, she went to explore the corridor which was long and gloomy, being lit by a single light controlled by a time-switch at some distance from her door. The bathroom was at the far end, evidently converted from an attic bedroom for it had low walls and a sloping roof. The antiquated bath, which rested on four legs, was marked with brown stains. The skylight above it was small and green with moss. Traces of some kind of mushroom growth could be seen on the walls. But at least the water was hot. As she turned on the tap it gurgled and spat and came out a dark brown colour, but it was almost boiling.

She ran it for a while to see if its colour would improve and, when it did not, she put in the plug and went back to the bedroom for her things. It was only as she was going out of her room for the second time that she saw the figure hanging behind the door.

She didn't scream; a fact she remembered afterwards with satisfaction. Then she realized that the swaying figure was an old dressing gown topped by a bath cap, the property no doubt, of her predecessor, Miss Crewe. All the same her heart was still thumping as she ran back to the bathroom. She looked warily around it and bolted the door before lowering herself into the hot caramel-coloured water.

CHAPTER THREE

Daylight streaming in through the cheap curtains woke her before seven o'clock. She lay looking around the bleak uncarpeted room, her eyes resting on each unlovely article of furniture in turn. For the first time in daylight she took in the rickety table, the worm-eaten chest of drawers. Defenceless, at the moment of waking, she was assailed by the memory of the other bedroom, with its fitted cupboards laboriously made, its concealed lighting, heavy curtains, thick white carpet still new enough to be shedding fluff. She was filled with cold empty misery. How could he, oh how could he?

She made herself shut out the memory. It was a new day, a new life. She would make something of this room, this life. She got up and went over to the window.

There were bars, she realised for the first time. She looked through them at a great expanse of green, from which mist was rising like steam from a rain forest. In the distance she could just make out the road she had travelled the night before. The view of the gravel turning space below was mainly obscured by the projecting roof of a lower room, but she could see the far corner where it joined the drive. There was a brown post or pillar which she had not noticed last night; it was surely rather dangerously placed there on the corner? She reached for her spectacles and saw that it was a figure dressed in brown, standing looking up at her window. It moved away with a curious, rather crab-like sideways walk, the figure of an old man, or a partly disabled one.

In the distance a bell clanged.

Only one table was laid in the corner of the dining room. At it was sitting Miss Fairbairn, Mrs Bland and a fair girl wearing a blue overall. As Ruth went in, she saw Miss Fairbairn turn to the girl and say something, upon which the girl immediately got up and, skirting the empty tables, went out through a side door which presumably led to the kitchens.

"Enjoy the peace and quiet when you can," Mrs Bland told Ruth after the preliminaries were over and they were finishing their toast and coffee. "It will be very different when the girls are back at supper time."

She glanced around the dining room. "It all looks very clean and shining," she remarked to Miss Fairbairn.

"So it should. The women were working on it practically all day yesterday."

Listening to them it struck Ruth that their roles were oddly reversed; thus it was Miss Fairbairn who played the traditional aloof headmistress role and Mrs Bland who was placatory. Stouter and altogether more comfortable to be with, she ought to have been the housekeeper. It seemed to be a case of bad casting.

"How is Michelle this morning?" Mrs Bland enquired.

"Better," Miss Fairbairn told her shortly.

"Michelle," Mrs Bland explained to Ruth, "is a French girl we have helping on the domestic staff – a kind of au pair arrangement, you know. You must meet her."

"I should like that – very much."

"Unfortunately it won't be possible," Miss Fairbairn cut in. "The domestic staff have completely different hours from the teaching staff."

She and Mrs Bland glanced at each other and a look of understanding passed between them. Then Mrs Bland turned back to Ruth. "Of course," she said. "How stupid of me; she'll be busy with cooking when you're free. I expect she'll make lots of friends in the kitchen anyway."

"I quite understand," Ruth said casually, having immediately made up her mind that she would get to know Michelle despite Esther Fairbairn. "I imagine it isn't easy to get domestic help out here."

"Practically impossible. Academic staff of course are two-a-penny, but domestics are pearls beyond price. It's a fearful task for poor Esther. But we are not alone in this. There isn't boarding school in the land that wouldn't gladly exchange half a dozen classicists for a really reliable cook."

Ruth laughed. Miss Fairbairn looked deliberately unamused. "The conditions of work here happen to be appalling," she cut in sharply. "Perhaps that has something to do with it."

"Oh, it has everything to do with it," Mrs Bland agreed. "We have the most antiquated kitchens in the whole of the British Isles. We should all have died of cholera long ago."

There was a sharp intake of breath from Miss Fairbairn, whereupon she added, "If it hadn't been for the immense care taken by Esther."

There was a moment's silence, then she went on, "But, seriously, of course, our main problem is that all the domestic offices are in the basement. There's not a glimmer of daylight down there and there are endless stairs and passages to contend with. It' s a real maze, more like catacombs than kitchens."

"Isn't that the kitchen through the side door?" Ruth asked.

"No, that's the servery. There is a staircase down from there to the kitchen. There's another way down through the baize door by the main staircase and another at the far end of the corridor opposite the staff study. It's all very confusing, which is just as well. When any poor soul comes for an interview we start them off in here and then lead them up and down so many staircases and corridors that they've no idea what level they are on, or that they're going to end up working entirely underground."

She laughed and stood up.

"And what are your plans, Miss Cassell?"

"I'd thought I'd explore the school this morning – the library and so on. I shall be rather dependent on it until my trunk comes with my books."

"But it's come," Mrs Bland said. "It came at least two days ago. I saw it in the cellar. Hasn't it been taken up, Esther?"

"I wouldn't know," the housekeeper said indifferently. "Presumably not, since Miss Cassell says so. I'll speak to Albert about it."

"How kind: I'm afraid I must leave you to your own devices today, Miss Cassell. I have interviews this morning with parents. If you want anything you need only approach Miss Fairbairn."

Ruth thanked her and glanced at Miss Fairbairn, who stared coldly back at her, a model of unapproachability.

After breakfast she wrote to her father. There could never again be any real communication between them, of course, but the outward courtesies would be maintained and certainly she didn't want him to worry about her. She wrote a brief and cheerful letter which revealed nothing of herself and then, since the trunk has still not appeared, decided to go in search of a letterbox.

It was drizzling as she walked down the drive. Rhododendron bushes dripped all around her and damp leaves stuck to her shoes. The biggest slugs she had ever seen lay at the roadside, black or brown and some with orange frills. She shuddered.

She made for the little hamlet she had noticed as she drove up the night before and after fifteen minutes' brisk walk came upon a cluster of houses in one of whose ivy-clad walls there nestled a letterbox. On the plate was written 'Little Polglaze'. The next collection was at noon. As she posted the letter an old man came along pushing his bicycle.

"You shouldn't have done that," he said, shaking his head.

"Why not?" she asked in surprise.

"T'aint a good box to be aposting of your letters," he said.

"Why not?" she asked again.

"The slugs do be eating of 'em," he explained, and continued on his way.

He was the only human being that she saw on her walk.

It was still only eleven when, driven back to school by gusts of wind and rain, she trudged up the sodden drive which was already beginning to resemble a river bed. What a place this is, she thought; wild, wet and stormy and inhabited by letter-eating slugs.

It was the need for more dry clothes that made her decide to go first to enquire about her trunk. She went to the dining room in the hope of seeing Miss Fairbairn. Nobody was about, so she crossed into the servery, where a woman busy sorting crockery told her that Miss Fairbairn was down below, indicating a door in the far wall.

She opened the door and went down a flight of steps. At the bottom was a series of kitchens and sculleries which seemed to be deserted. She went through another door and found herself in a passage. As she walked along it she noticed that the air was stuffy with a faintly smoky smell which she later identified as coke fumes, the smell of boiler rooms.

Mrs Bland had not been exaggerating when she described the school cellars as catacombs; there was a bewildering maze of corridors, passageways and tiny store rooms. She decided that it was hopeless to wander around trying to find the housekeeper and had just turned back when she saw the French girl whom she had glimpsed at breakfast time.

"Excuse me," she said. "I'm Ruth Cassell. I'm new here and I'm looking for Miss Fairbairn."

The girl's face lit up; it had seemed heavy and brooding, but was now suddenly attractive. "I'm Michelle Duron," she said and held out her hand. "How do you do?"

The careful speech and formal continental handshake were bizarre in these cellars.

"Mrs Bland said we must meet," Ruth said on an impulse. "Perhaps you would like to come and have coffee with me one evening in my room?"

"I should like it very much. I am on duty until nine o'clock but could come after that."

"Good. Let's say tomorrow night then? Though how we'll manage to make it I can't imagine! There's no kettle or..."

They were interrupted by the sound of Michelle's voice being called. It was Miss Fairbairn's voice and it was alarmingly close at hand. They both jumped guiltily.

"You are needed in the linen room," the housekeeper told the French girl sharply.

When Michelle had gone, she turned to Ruth with undisguised hostility. "Miss Cassell," she said, "to what do we owe the honour of your visit to the dungeons which we mere domestics inhabit?"

"I came to ask about my trunk," Ruth began.

"I will enquire," Miss Fairbairn said and turned away.

Ruth followed her down corridors, the atmosphere growing dustier and stuffier all the time. Esther Fairbairn stopped outside a door. "Albert," she called softly.

The door opened, revealing piles of coke, and a man crept out. He was wearing brown overalls tied round the middle with string and he shuffled towards them with the sideways walk of the figure she had seen looking up at her window that morning. His head was twisted to one side, but it was his face that caught her attention. It was such a gentle face, sad and resigned.

"Where is Miss Cassell's trunk?" Miss Fairbairn asked.

He nodded and pointed up at the ceiling and then in a surprisingly soft, cultured voice, he said, "I have taken it up to her room."

Ruth thanked him, wondering how he had achieved this feat, and then as Miss Fairbairn was already walking away, quickly followed her, afraid of being lost. The housekeeper took her by a different route this time and then, stopping suddenly, said, "You go along there until you come to some steps which come out opposite the staff room. That, if I may say so, is the department to which *you* belong. We each have our domain, do we not?"

Without waiting for a reply, she turned and walked away.

Ruth continued on the way she had been shown, but it was not a direct route and before she reached the stairs the light went out. For a moment she panicked, imagining all kinds of horrors brushing her face, hands reaching out at her. At last she came to the stairs and at the top found the baize door which led out into the linoleum-covered main school corridor. She stood for a moment panting with relief. Then, telling herself not to be absurd, and feeling reassured by the normality of the school corridor, she crossed over to the door marked staff room, and went in.

The room was divided by an archway, at the far side of which there were desks and tables ranged round the walls. At one a young woman was sitting busy with books and papers. She looked up as Ruth came in.

"Oh, I'm sorry," Ruth said, standing awkwardly in the doorway. "I didn't realise there was anybody here. I'm new and I've come to teach history."

The woman got up. "Well, come in," she said. "I'm Helen Rhodes, by the way. And don't apologise; you've as much right here as I have – if right is the word for the appalling obligation to work in here."

She was slight and elegant, her dark brown hair drawn back into a pleat. Her brown eyes were heavy-lidded, making her expression mildly disdainful, but not unpleasantly so. All the same, Ruth felt immediately younger and untidier. She pushed her hair back off her face and stammered slightly when she spoke.

"I thought I'd just come and settle myself in here and start preparing a few lessons," she explained.

"First job?"

"Yes, I'm afraid so."

"Don't be afraid. It's as good a place as any to make all your mistakes in. Nobody could hold it against you here."

She looked around the room. "That's where your predecessor sat," she said, indicating an adjoining desk, "so I should help yourself to it. Unless you're superstitious, of course."

Ruth laughed. "I gather she wasn't much good."

"She was disastrous! She only had to set foot in a form room for bedlam to break out. In fact it broke out in advance, such is the sense of pleasurable anticipation of the young."

"Don't – I'm frightened enough already."

It was a relief to admit it, it was a relief to talk to someone normal.

"Well, everybody's frightened at first; after all, you're outnumbered by about twenty to one. But just don't let them see it, that's all that matters. I suppose you did some kind of teacher training?"

"No. I was going to, after taking my degree, but – well, I changed my plans."

"A very good thing too. It's all rubbish, this idea of teaching people to teach. They stuff you with theories and you read books on child psychology and when you actually get into the classroom it's no good at all. The kids haven't read those child psychology books and don't know the theories, so they react in all the wrong ways. Besides, in a crisis you haven't time to work out the right way to handle them; you've just got to react instinctively. A moment's hesitation and you're lost. They've got you. Your best guide is a strong instinct of self-preservation."

"You make it sound like all-out war."

"It is. Anyway at first. And you must win it You must win within the first two weeks and then after that you can relax. You even get to like them. It's odd really. But get the upper hand first."

"I'll try. I don't want to go the way of Miss Crewe."

"Well, you know, I have a theory," Helen Rhodes said, leaning back in her chair and stretching out her legs in front of her. They were long, slender legs and she balanced her heels carefully on the floor so that her sharp ankle bones just touched each other. "Which is that on every staff there must be a fixed proportion of people who can't keep order. It must be a kind of safety valve. Well, we're a very small staff, so we just need one and we already have Puddles – that's the name by which the children call Miss Pool, the geography mistress."

"Tell me about the others – that is if I'm not interrupting your work."

She looked around the staff room. "Starting over by the door, there sits an ancient mathematician by the name of Enders. She's an emaciated old crone who not only does not teach the New Maths, but has not even heard of it."

"That must be a great relief to the parents."

"The joy with which parents bemused, by New Maths in other schools, discover that here we still do old-fashioned sums is quite pitiful to behold."

"And next to her?"

"Next to her is the other Miss Enders, her sister. She's younger and fat and teaches what is laughingly called Science, without benefit of laboratory or equipment. The children distinguish them by calling them the Big End and Little End."

Ruth laughed. "And next to the Big End?"

"Then we have poor Puddles, who struggles with geography. Then you, of course, then me. My subject is English, though such is the nature of the place that I was originally appointed to teach French and junior Latin. Then we acquired a French master and I reverted to my own subject."

"You have masters here?"

"No, the experiment was not a success. After a year of misery inflicted upon him by our little girls, the French master left to become a monk"

"And now?"

"Now French is taught by the local vicar's widow. She is deaf and not very sociable so you won't see her in here much. Mrs Crago, she's called."

"But how does she manage to teach if she's deaf?"

"Oh, she has her own method – not exactly the approved modern method of course. The children recite verbs and do vocabulary tests and are not allowed to ask questions. But she does let them sing; she teaches them a French song and then turns off her hearing aid and lets the girls give vent. The noise is incredible."

"And that's the entire staff?"

"Well, everybody who uses this study. On the non-academic side there is an appalling old biddy called Mrs Hamilton-Smythe who teaches games. You can't mistake her. She's offensively clad in shorts and tee shirts quite unsuitable to her age and size. The music staff are mostly part-time. Domestic Science is catered for by a visiting lady originally employed to mend the linen, I believe."

"And Mrs Bland is a Classicist?"

"That's right. She takes Latin throughout the school and some VIth Form Greek. She teaches Divinity too for no particular reason except it's what Heads tend to do." Her voice softened and quite lost its sardonic tone. "She's a marvellous person actually. There's nothing else one can say about her. She can teach anything to anybody. She's what people call a born teacher and believe me they *are* born, not made."

"And Miss Fairbairn?"

Helen Rhodes' voice changed and her expression hardened. "She is the most sickening creature that ever blighted the earth and it's high time somebody killed her," she said.

She laughed at the shock on Ruth's face.

"Well," she said defensively, "I mean, to see somebody of Mrs Bland's calibre subjected to a bitch like that..."

"But does she have to be subjected? I mean, Miss Fairbairn's only the housekeeper, isn't she?"

"As if that had anything to do with it! In relationships like that one is always subjected to the other, but it has nothing to do with jobs or status."

She changed the subject abruptly.

"And what brings you here? A young hopeful like you offering yourself up at this New Lowood? Why not some exciting new Comprehensive? Or if it must be a boarding school, why not a good public school?"

"Just what my father said," Ruth remarked in surprise.

"What does he do, your father?"

"He's a Professor of History at London University."

"So they live in London, your parents? That's where your home is?"

Ruth hesitated, then "Yes, that's right," she said.

Helen Rhodes did not pursue it. "Well, you've certainly chosen a crummy old place to make your academic debut," she said, "but no doubt you have your reasons."

"Why do parents send their children here?" Ruth asked to divert the conversation from herself.

Helen laughed. "You may well ask," she said. "It's a lot to do with the eleven plus. Parents don't want their children to go to a Secondary Modern when they fail it. We don't have an entrance exam, so it suits the needs of rich parents with not very bright children."

"And what about exam results?"

"Well, perhaps I did paint rather a bleak picture. Of course it's pretty hopeless for any child who's scientifically minded, but if we get one gifted on the arts side, it has as good a chance as any. The classes are small and in the Sixth Form they get individual attention. We sent a girl to Cambridge to read Classics last year. The library is pretty awful, but Mrs Bland lends her own books and I use the County library. It's all very improvised but I honestly don't think any clever child is held back."

"Except the scientists?"

"Well, that's true of a lot of girls' schools and Mrs Bland sometimes arranges with the council for some of them to go to other institutions for lab work. She's by no means unscrupulous –"

"You like her, don't you?"

"Oh, yes, I've a lot of time for Mrs Bland. She may talk flippantly but she's deadly serious underneath. And the place has vastly improved since she came."

"I wonder why she stays here?"

Helen shrugged, "Who knows? Maybe it just suits her. She does a fantastic amount of teaching. If she was Head of a better school, she'd be administering all the time, which she'd hate. The barmy thing about the teaching profession is that the best teachers get promoted and the kids lose a good teacher and gain a poor administrator."

"So you think she'll stay here and try to build it up?"

"Yes, she might do it too. She's managed to entrap you, for example. I expect she interviewed you in London, and you had no idea what kind of establishment you were coming to?"

Ruth shrugged. "I didn't even know such establishments existed. You make it sound a pretty appalling prospect."

"It is," Helen Rhodes said simply. "You'll be stuck up there on that awful top landing with Puddles for company. Dear Esther will make sure you see nothing of Mrs Bland. I just hope you don't mind loneliness – because there's nobody for company here."

"There's you," Ruth said with a laugh.

"Oh, no, there isn't," Helen Rhodes told her coolly. "Don't count on me for companionship. I come here, do what I'm paid to do and go. I do not get involved – ever."

Rebuffed, Ruth could think of no reply. Eventually she said, "I suppose you mean that at a better school you'd be obliged to..."

"We all have our reasons for staying here," Helen interrupted. "It suits me as it suits you. It suits the Enders because they're too old to change and nobody would have them anyway. Poor Puddles is still young – well, she was born middle-aged and harassed, but you know what I mean – but she wouldn't survive a week in a proper school. And how would deaf Mrs Crago cope in a language lab?"

She stretched and yawned, and glanced at her watch.

"I must be off," she said. "End of gossip."

She put on her coat, knotted a scarf neatly round her neck, said goodbye and left. Ruth followed her out of the staff room and went upstairs to unpack her trunk.

CHAPTER FOUR

All that afternoon Ruth heard the sounds of children returning, cars drawing up on the gravel, doors slamming, farewells being shouted. The corridors began to echo with what sounded, at a distance, like a mob surging mindlessly up and down. The silence was sudden and unnatural when, after a bell rang, they all withdrew to the dormitories to unpack. There was still nobody about later as she went downstairs to the staff room.

Sitting by the fire was a small abject figure which she guessed to be Miss Pool. The little body was encased in brown wool; above the dark brown skirt was a beige jumper from whose sleeves bony hands projected and were held up nervously to the fire. The fingers were so thin that it seemed that the light shone through them, giving them a pinkly transparent look like the paws of a mouse. Miss Pool's face was pale, almost putty-coloured and its lack of chin and tiny mouth added to the mousey look; her nervous little eyes darted about as if looking for a hole to run to. Her hair was mouse-coloured and looped back from her face into a straggly bun, a kind of hairy little sausage in the nape of her neck.

She smiled weakly at Ruth as she came in, "I'm Mary Pool," she said apologetically.

Ruth introduced herself and sat down on the other side of the fire. It was an old-fashioned grate with a big cast iron hood. All the time they talked Miss Pool fiddled with the fire, plying it with tiny pieces of coal as if her life depended on maintaining it in a black and smoky pyramid.

"It's nice to have a fire. It looks so homely," Ruth said and then wondered at herself for choosing such a word.

"Yes. Yes. It is warmer at this end," Miss Pool agreed, and Ruth realised that this room, like the Head's study, was divided by an archway and from an almost independent room on the other side.

"It's nearly time for supper," Miss Pool went on, glancing at her watch after pulling back a baggy sleeve to reveal the thinnest and boniest wrist that Ruth had ever seen.

"Is everyone back?" Ruth asked. "I haven't seen any of the staff yet. I've been in my room unpacking."

"Yes. I've seen them all." She hesitated. "Would you like me to tell you about them?" she asked nervously. And, sensing that Miss Pool would find it easier to have a subject to retail, Ruth said that she would.

"I'll just make sure that there is nobody in the other end," Miss Pool said, getting up and walking under the archway to look around the other end of the room. Ruth wondered what libellous statements she was about to make, that required such secrecy.

"There is Miss Claire and Miss Ada Enders," Miss Pool said. "They're both very clever. They teach Maths and Science. They are very good at keeping order too," she added wistfully.

She stared at the fire for a moment and then began compulsively arranging the coal.

Wherever there was a tiny glow or a flicker of flame she extinguished it with a small black ingot.

"Then there is Mrs Hamilton-Smythe, who takes all the gym and games. She is Head of House too. She comes of a very good family."

She spoke with satisfaction, as if the consoling existence of the great and powerful made her own life easier to bear.

"Mrs Rhodes lives out. She's very capable is Mrs Rhodes."

"Oh, I've met Helen Rhodes. I didn't realise she was married."

"Oh yes. She's very modern."

Ruth could not think of an appropriate reply, so she said, "That leaves the two of us – on the top landing."

"I'm glad you've come. After Miss Crewe went I was so afraid I'd be up there alone."

She looked around the room, got up and checked that there was still nobody in the far end and added, "She took an overdose you know. We don't talk about it."

"No! I'd no idea!" Ruth exclaimed, shocked. "You mean she killed herself?"

"Oh, no, nothing like that," Miss Pool said. She spoke more firmly now, her confidence reinforced by the impression her remark had made. "They took her to hospital, Mrs Bland did."

"But she didn't come back to teach?"

"No, she never came back," Miss Pool said. "She had a nervous breakdown," she added enviously.

She stared into the fire, as if aware that her own existence would be allowed no such dramatic interlude.

"It's my first job," Ruth said, trying to distract her. "I'd be so grateful for any help you can give me."

"Oh, you'll be all right," Miss Pool said flatly. "You've got character."

Ruth was spared the need to reply by the arrival of the rest of the staff, led by Mrs Bland who first greeted Miss Pool, who flushed and looked down, and then introduced Ruth to the others. Formalities over, she led the way to the dining room.

The girls were standing at the tables and watched in silence as their few members of staff processed up to the top table on a dais at the far end of the room. They were already wearing school uniform; Ruth had a vague impression of faces, of brown hair and green tunics and wondered if she would ever distinguish between them, even with her spectacles on. She was aware of a hundred-and-eighty-pairs of eyes upon her as the children silently assessed this latest addition to their staff.

Mrs Bland stood at one end of the staff table, Miss Fairbairn the other. Too late Ruth found herself silting next to the housekeeper. As Mrs Bland said grace, Ruth resolved not to be intimidated by Esther Fairbairn. She told herself firmly that if Miss Fairbairn chose to be rude she would be rude back and answer indifference with indifference. People like that should not be placated.

She was sitting with her back to the hall, so could hear, but not see, the girls. "They're still subdued," Miss Ada Enders remarked as they ate their soup. "They get noisier as they settle in."

Two things surprised Ruth; one was the excellence of the meal and the other was the deference shown by the staff to Miss Fairbairn. Mrs Hamilton-Smythe was positively obsequious.

At the far end of the table Mrs Bland and Miss Claire Enders were discussing the career of one of their girls who had just come down from University.

"The trouble with girls straight from college," Miss Fairbairn said looking straight at Ruth, "is that they think they know everything and in fact know nothing."

"Oh, I don't know," Ruth began to protest.

"Indeed you don't," Esther Fairbairn cut in. "They may be *clever,*" she went on, emphasising the word in such a way as to make it clear that she used it as a term of abuse, "but they have no maturity of knowledge of the world."

"How I do agree!" Mrs Hamilton-Smythe put in. "In my view it is far too easy to go there nowadays – at our expense, needless to say. It was different in our day."

"I could have gone to the university," the housekeeper said with sudden bitterness, "but my father could not afford it. A clergyman's salary didn't run to it in those days."

Ruth looked at her with sudden remorse; tout comprendre, c'est tout pardoner.

"And naturally my brother had to be the one to go, although he was less academically gifted than myself."

"How dreadful!" Ruth exclaimed.

Esther Fairbairn turned on her with icy fury. "You will please not impugn my father's judgement. I have abided by it and I will not have it criticised by some girl straight from college."

Ruth remembered her resolution not to be intimidated – and broke it. It was all very well, she thought after accepting the insult in silence, but you can't be rude to somebody almost twice your age and that in the company of other old people. It would be different if I was alone with her, she excused herself as she sat with burning cheeks. Nobody took any notice. So this was why they feared Miss Fairbairn – for her uncontrollable temper. For the rest of the meal the housekeeper ignored her.

There was coffee to be had in the staff room afterwards, but she went straight upstairs, unable to face them. She couldn't take any more. It was a wretched, miserable place inhabited by awful people and she dearly wished she had never come. The only two people she might have turned to were Mrs Bland, whose position placed her out of bounds, and Helen Rhodes, who had warned her off. She remembered that cool rejection now and felt a shiver of loneliness. In the distance she could hear the hum of children's voices and the thought that tomorrow, alone and outnumbered, she would have to face a whole classroom full of them, with their watchful eyes always upon her, increased her sense of foreboding. The confidence and excitement at starting a new life, which she had felt on the train, had quite deserted her. She went to bed aware that never in her life had she felt so miserable.

CHAPTER FIVE

It went better than she had feared. She was aware of being dangerously outnumbered and sometimes had an ignoble desire to placate the children who were, after all, much more agreeable company than the staff, but she followed Helen Rhodes' advice, was determinedly strict and found to her surprise, on that first day, that they did what she told them without question. Perhaps they were just biding their time, but more worrying was the realisation that nothing she had studied in the past three years was going to be of the slightest use to her in the days ahead.

She was sitting at the rickety table, surrounded by books borrowed from the library and purloined from the textbook storeroom, trying to plan tomorrow's lessons, when there was a knock at the door and Michelle came in. She looked guiltily over her shoulder and said, "Nobody saw me, I think."

"What does it matter if they do?"

Michelle shrugged her shoulders and said nothing. Then she produced out of a shopping basket, which she had carefully covered with newspaper, a small kettle, two mugs, half a bottle of milk and a box of matches.

"It was agreeable to take them without Miss Fairbairn knowing," she said when Ruth thanked her. "I really enjoyed doing it."

Ruth laughed, "Well, you've certainly thought of everything," she said as Michelle took two teaspoons out of the bottom of the basket. "I shall go shopping on Saturday and then you won't need to steal for me any more."

"The children have lessons on Saturday mornings and the shop in Polglaze is shut in the afternoon," Michelle told her.

"What a place! However do you stand it? Couldn't you get a job in London? Your English is so good."

"Thank you," Michelle said politely and watched in silence as Ruth made the coffee and lit the gas fire.

It was the antique kind which spluttered alarmingly when she put a match to it. They watched as the curved flutes began to glow yellow and orange in the flames, the spluttering stopped and the fire hissed quietly to itself.

"It's comforting, isn't it?" Ruth remarked. "A live flame, the next best thing to an open fire. They don't allow ones like this any more. Against safety rules or something. I'm sorry there are no comfortable chairs," she added as they settled themselves down on the floor by the gas fire.

"It's awful, your room," Michelle said simply.

"What's yours like?"

"Worse."

"Where is it?"

"In the cellar. It is smokily."

"I bet it is. Why ever are you down there?"

"It is where the domestic staff are. Albert sleeps next to the coke. Miss Fairbairn is on a landing halfway between the cellar and the ground floor. I am the only other one sleeping there. The rest go home at night."

"But it's *awful*."

"I suppose they think it is convenient."

"Couldn't you have had a job as an assistant? Not necessarily in this school, but anywhere?"

Michelle shook her head. "No," she said. "It must be here."

Then she seemed to fear she had been rude and went on, "I thought that I *would* be assistante here. It was surprising to me to find what my work was."

"What do you do?"

"It is heavy work. The kitchens – well, you know what they are like. Then everything has to be carried up – the crates for the milk bottles, everything like that. But I am quite strong."

"But..."

"I am here for a year and I will bear it. I will not tell them at home. But when I have finished I will never, never come again to England."

"But, Michelle, you mustn't think that this place is typical. You really should go somewhere else."

"It is impossible." She hesitated. "I will tell you this and then you will please forget, yes?"

"Yes."

"Very recently, my father died. My mother when I was young. Just before he died he had had an invitation for me to come here for a year, which he wanted me to do. Very much he wished me to speak English because my mother was English."

"Yes, I quite understand that. But–"

"It seemed a good idea to come. I thought as an assistant. After my father died our lawyer, who is also a friend of the family who sees to everything, says to me to come just the same. It seems an opportunity to make better my English and a good change for me, because naturally I am very sad at this time."

"Yes, yes, I know," Ruth said with feeling, forgetting for a moment that this was not in fact her own predicament.

"You too have no parents?"

Ruth hesitated. "I am alone," she said.

"I am invited here," Michelle said, "because Mrs Bland is my mother's sister."

Ruth stared at her. "She's your *aunt?*" she exclaimed. "And she lets you be treated like a drudge and kept in that awful cellar and bossed about?"

Michelle smiled and took her hand. "Don't," she said, "I have said – I will bear it, but when the year is finished, I go away and I never come back. But I will not complain or they will be upset. I do not wish them to know at home what it is like for me here."

She had a very determined chin, Ruth observed.

"Well, I think it's dreadful," she began, "And if I were you–"

"You are not," Michelle said firmly. "Besides, my father was pleased for me to come because for years the family had been, what do you say? – like strangers... ?"

"Estranged?"

"Yes, my mother and my aunt. After marrying a Frenchman my mother never came back to England, so he was pleased to have this invitation to me and I know he would wish me to come."

"But not to stay when it is like this."

"It is better now that you have come."

Deliberately she changed the subject.

"What will you do to make better this room?" she asked. "It is a big and good shape. You could make it much more comfortable. Do you sew?"

"No, I'm hopeless at it."

"Then I will help you. I like to sew. No," when Ruth began to protest. "I should like it, please. My own room is no good to improve."

She kept her word. They went into Truro together the next Saturday afternoon and bought material, which Michelle made into a cover for the trunk and, having stolen from under Miss Fairbairn's very nose some old pillows, made cushions to match. Together they rifled junk shops for lamps and Michelle made new shades for them. She bought a rag mat in the market for a shilling and brought it back in triumph.

"Look how well it is made, Ruth, and the colours are they not beautiful? It will be better for sitting on in front of the gas fire."

"It does have a few bald patches."

"They are not a problem. I have pieces of material I can cut up and weave in."

Ruth watched in amazement as Michelle tackled in an evening a task which she herself would have struggled with for weeks. Her fingers worked with equally swift competence on cloth, wood or metal, restoring order, bestowing elegance. All the chores which she herself would have found tedious, Michelle took delight in. It was all wrong that this talented, creative person should be toiling away in the dungeon. Even for one year.

"I wish you'd make something for yourself, Michelle," she remarked one evening, after the French girl had been sitting by the fire sewing, while she herself marked books at the desk.

"Ah, you know my thoughts! When I am paid next week I am going to buy material for a coat. I have seen some beautiful, deep red cloth, very good, pure wool and not expensive."

That was another thing about Michelle: she had an eye for a bargain.

"And I shall use you for a model because we are the same size and shape."

So at odd times in the evenings, she stood while Michelle, her mouth full of pins, arranged the fabric on her, adjusted, tacked and snipped until the roll of cloth was transformed, in ten days, into a beautiful coat. To Ruth, who had no such skills, it seemed nothing short of miraculous.

"For your modelling I am most grateful," Michelle told her.

"Rubbish," Ruth told her, glancing around her transformed room. "I am the one who should be grateful."

But she knew it was really for Michelle's friendship that she was grateful. For if she had found the girls easier than she'd expected, the staff were much worse. They were uniformly unfriendly. She suspected they would have been different had it not been for the poison injected into the atmosphere by Esther Fairbairn. Her one ally might have been Helen Rhodes but she did exactly as she had said she would; came to the school, did the job she was paid to do and went away again.

So apart from Michelle she talked to almost nobody except the children, and with them she was still on her guard, deliberately acting a part. She had always loved acting and now created for herself the role of a zealous young schoolmistress. She brainwashed herself into believing that if she issued an order it was quite impossible for them to disobey her. She found, to her surprise, that this conviction carried itself into her voice and was obeyed. It's all just an act, she thought to herself; it has nothing to do with training or methods or anything.

She had been there over a month when she woke up early, feeling ill, felt worse during breakfast and during prayers she fainted. They got her out of the chapel and into the private house guest room opposite. There Miss Crowe, the nurse, laid her down on the bed, covered her with a blanket, gave her a hot water bottle and left her to rest.

"You're worn out," she said. "You take my advice and have the day off. Children are nasty creatures; if they see you're not well they take advantage."

All the adults here, Ruth reflected, are uniformly nasty and suspicious. She was feeling better now; pleasantly light-headed and drowsy after fainting. It was very pleasant to lie and drift off to sleep.

She felt a hand on her forehead and, to her surprise, heard Mrs Bland's voice murmuring, "Poor little bird, not so strong as she thought." The hand strayed from her hair, stroking her face. Ruth lay quite still, dreadfully embarrassed, and pretended to be asleep.

She didn't hear the door open but guessed that somebody had come in by the way the hand moved abruptly away. Then she heard Esther Fairbairn's whisper in a voice that was almost a hiss, "So, so, this is where you are. This is what is going on, is it?"

"Keep your voice down, Esther," she heard Mrs Bland say very quietly. "Miss

Cassell is asleep, as you see."

They were both over by the door now.

"How dare you tell me to be quiet? How much longer will this go on?"

"Nothing is going on," Mrs Bland said wearily. "I am of course concerned for my staff."

"And where would you be without me?"

"Esther, you know I fully acknowledge what you do. I couldn't begin to run this place without you. We depend on you utterly, you know that."

There was a pause and then Mrs Bland repeated, with a humility that astonished Ruth so much that she nearly opened her eyes.

Esther Fairbairn replied, "Yes. Yes, I do; it's just that sometimes I need to be told."

Mrs Bland did not reply. The silence was intense. The atmosphere electric. Then, after what seemed a very long time, Ruth heard the door open and close quietly and she knew she was alone at last.

She got up quickly and went downstairs. Whatever the nurse had said about the children taking advantage of you if you were ill, she would feel safer in the classroom than up in the Head's private quarters with Esther Fairbairn on the prowl.

She muddled through the day somehow or other and at the end of lessons went up to her room to work quietly. She was interrupted later by a tap on her door.

It was Miss Pool who had brought up her supper on a tray.

"Working, Miss Cassell?" she asked in surprise, her pale face expressing horror. "We thought you would be in bed."

"I'm better," Ruth told her. "I think I was just a bit overtired. It was very kind of you to bring the tray up – have a cup of coffee while I eat?"

Miss Pool sat down and looked unhappily at the gas fire as if she would have liked to stoke it. Her hands fluttered about nervously as she spoke.

"You saw your letter? I put it on the tray under a plate."

"Yes, thank you. I'll read it later."

It was only from Alastair; it would keep.

"I only saw it just now. You see the letters do sometimes go up a bit late."

"Who puts them up on the rack?" Ruth asked, knowing how Puddles liked explaining things.

"The post is taken in by the Secretary if she's there in the morning, but often Mrs Bland sees to the afternoon post herself. And sorts it in her study – I've seen her – so I suppose if she is engaged it just waits until later."

"That explains the delays."

"She sees to nearly everything, Mrs Bland does. She's wonderful, isn't she? I think that's what makes it such a happy school."

Ruth glanced at her to see if the irony was intended. But Miss Pool went on,

"We all get on so well. I mean everybody was asking how you were. They were very sorry you were ill this morning. You must take care to keep your strength up."

"Oh, I'm all right. How are things downstairs?"

"All right, I think. Oh, that little French maid nearly had a very bad accident."

Ruth put down her knife and fork and stared at her. "What happened to her?"

"It was in the tower," Miss Pool said, talking more confidently now that she had a near tragedy to relate. "You know we are allowed to take groups of children up? It's the science and maths staff mostly; they measure heights or something. And of course there are excellent views."

"Yes, I've heard that," Ruth interrupted. "But what happened to her?"

"Who? Oh, you mean the French girl. Well, you know the tower isn't very safe – that's why the girls aren't allowed up unsupervised. Mrs Bland is very particular about safety. Well, apparently the French girl took it into her head to go up this evening. I don't know why; we never go up at night. Foreigners are funny, aren't they? Well, some of the stairs are broken and she nearly fell It's a spiral staircase, you see, and very narrow, and if you fall you drop down a very long way. She would have been killed."

"How do you know about it? Did she tell you?"

"Goodness no, I'm sure we shouldn't have known anything about it but Mrs Fox from the Lodge happened to be at the top of the drive – round the back you know – and she heard the girl call out. She ran in but by that time the girl was down again. She was quite all right, only just a bit frightened."

"Poor thing!"

"It'll teach her not to be so careless," Miss Pool remarked with the casual heartlessness of one who is used to being callously treated herself.

"But she could have been killed."

"Yes, she seemed to think that Miss Fairbairn had wanted her to go up. I suppose she didn't understand. Her English isn't very good apparently."

"But it is excellent. She'd never misunderstand a thing like that and she understands even better than she speaks."

Miss Pool looked at her in surprise. "Do you know her, then?" she asked.

Ruth hesitated, and decided not to risk their friendship being reported back to Esther Fairbairn who would undoubtedly wreak her displeasure on Michelle.

"No," she said. "I only meant that we all understand foreign languages better than we speak them, so presumably she does too."

"I suppose so," she sighed. "I don't understand any foreign languages myself."

There was a silence in which Miss Pool was clearly bringing herself round to saying she would go now.

"You've made your room very nice," she said.

Just in time Ruth stopped herself saying that Michelle had helped her. There was another silence.

"Well," Miss Pool said, smiling nervously as she got up.

"Thank you for bringing up the tray. It was very kind of you."

"I'll let you rest now and read your letter. And if you need anything, you know..." still talking she managed to edge out of the room.

Ruth didn't open Alastair's letter. He had already written once suggesting he might come down to see her. Presumably he'd got the address from her father. Not wanting to hurt him but equally not wanting any visitors from the past, with their painful reminders of how life had once been, she had replied kindly but firmly discouraging him from coming here. She would reply in the same way to this one when she had time.

Now she had more important things to do; taking the tray so that she would have an excuse to be seen in the kitchen area, she went downstairs.

Michelle's basement room was near to the boiler room. It was small, had a tiny window high in the wall and was more like a cell than a bedroom. Michelle was sitting by the gas fire; she looked up in surprise when Ruth came in.

"I was coming to see you," she said. "Are you better? What was the matter? What's the tray for?"

Ruth laughed. "It's my excuse for coming down here in case I meet Miss Fairbairn."

"It's safe. She's upstairs with the Head. She'll be there until she goes to bed."

"Tell me about your accident in the tower," Ruth asked.

"Ah, you've heard," Michelle remarked with a hopeless shrug.

"Puddles told me, but I'd like to know what really happened."

"Well, you know Miss Fairbairn has the key to the tower and if anyone wants to go up they go to her for it?"

"Yes."

"This evening she comes to me and says she has to go up the tower and get some things left there by one of the classes, but she is called away to see the Head, so please will I run up instead. So she takes me to the bottom of the tower, unlocks the door and says she will leave me to put the key back in her room when I am down again."

Ruth nodded. "But wasn't she afraid some of the kids might climb up after you? There's always such a fuss about the tower being kept locked."

"She said it was quite safe as they were all in prep. It is a time of day when nobody is about, you know."

"That's true. Then?"

"Then she goes away. The light is on, so I do not think about anything except to run up the stairs, at least not quite run as they are steep and narrow. There is a rail at the side to hold."

"So what happened?"

"You know how everywhere in this building we have these nasty time

30

switches?"

Ruth nodded, remembering her first experience of getting lost in the dark in the basement.

"Well, I was nearly at the top when the light went off. I stopped, just holding on to the little rail. Then I thought there will be another light at the top and was just going on again, when there was a sudden flame."

She looked at Ruth and there was horror in her eyes. "Ruth," she said. "I do not exaggerate, I promise. That flame saved my life."

"What flame?"

"You know the big bonfire; where the gardener has been burning the leaves? Well, it was burning very slowly, but the wind started tonight and must have suddenly made it go up in big flames."

Ruth nodded. "Yes, I know. It flares up sometimes. I've seen it."

"That is the expression. It flared up. By the light I saw very plainly and I saw that the stairs I was going up stopped and suddenly there were no stairs at all. And the rail was broken too."

She stopped and Ruth saw again the look of horror. "Truly it was just a big black hole. Without the bonfire I should have gone straight down. And then there is nothing, you know, except great pieces of stones below."

Ruth took her hand. "Try not to imagine it," was all she could think of saying.

"Yes, I know. It was just a silly accident and I suppose Miss Fairbairn feels as awful about it as I do."

Ruth was silent for a moment, and then said slowly, "She's giving out that you misunderstood her and that she didn't mean you to go up. Is it possible?"

Michelle looked astonished. "Why ever should she say that?" she asked.

"Guilty conscience?" Ruth suggested.

"Yes, I suppose she felt afterwards that she was to blame."

"Which she was! And if you'd been killed she would simply have said that you helped yourself to the key and she knew nothing about it. Nobody would have known the truth."

"But she has no reason to want to harm me," Michelle objected.

"Oh, I'm sure she didn't *intend* to have anything like that happen," Ruth said with a conviction she did not feel.

"After all," Michelle added wryly, "I am quite useful to her."

Ruth smiled at her. "Well, you're even more useful to me, so don't go having any more accidents." She yawned. "We've both had a bit of a day, what with one thing and another, so I think an early night would be a good idea, don't you?"

She'd said good-night, and was going upstairs, when it struck her that with everything in the basement quiet and Miss Fairbairn and the Head closeted together upstairs, this was a chance to go and look at the tower, to view the scene of the crime, because that was how she was beginning to think of this accident.

She switched on the light outside the tower door and tried the handle. The door was locked. What else had she expected, she asked herself, as the turned back towards the staircase, leaving the light to turn itself off.

Except that it didn't. Glancing back she saw that it still shone, a strip of light under the door. This was no timer switch, as Michelle had supposed; it was a perfectly ordinary light which could only have been turned off deliberately.

Quickly she turned it off and made her way back, her heart thumping, to the safety of her room.

Once there, she sat for a while by the gas fire, trying to make sense of it, trying to think what she should do. There was no point in worrying Michelle when there was nothing either of them could do about it. Yet she should surely be told if she really was in danger, inexplicable though it all seemed.

She picked up Alastair's letter; there was something reassuring about the old familiar handwriting and she seemed to hear his voice as she read his words, the voice of sanity, normality, in this mad and frightening world. He wanted to come to see her. It would only be a brief visit; evidently they were working him hard at the approved school where he had chosen to spend a year to see if probation work really was his thing.

She was taken aback by the rush of joy she felt at the idea of seeing him again. She must have been mistaken when she thought she didn't want to see anyone from her old life; it would be such a relief now to talk to somebody who knew her as a real person, not just the history mistress at Polglaze School, and to share with him her anxiety about Michelle, knowing that he would listen and understand.

They had always got on well, she and Alastair, alone or among friends. It was only when he came home with her, that things had been difficult. When her father was there, Alastair seemed much less adult, went all awkward and immature; like a schoolboy in the presence of his Headmaster, he was over-anxious to please and kept calling her father 'Sir' which embarrassed both her and her father. She remembered with shame how they used to admit this to each other after he'd gone and even laughed a bit about him, though her father would say, "He's such a nice chap. But I do wish he wouldn't call me 'Sir', it makes me feel so very old."

None of that was important now. It would just be the two of them alone together, talking. And making love, she thought, shivering with remembered pleasure. He was always careful with her, he kept the rules: thus far and no further. Looking back now she thought it must have been frustrating for him, all the foreplay that only led to more foreplay. Nice for her, but frustrating for him. She'd said so once, but he'd just kissed her and said quietly, "You don't take risks with people you love."

All this reminiscing won't do, she told herself firmly as she settled down at the rickety table to work on tomorrow's lessons: notes on the French Revolution for the Lower Fifth, notes for the double period with the Sixth Form on the causes of the Great War and a set of books to be marked on the Norman Conquest to be returned to the Lower Fourth at nine o'clock tomorrow morning.

CHAPTER SIX

The staff meeting was coming to an end.

"Just two more matters," Mrs Bland was saying. "Firstly, you'll be glad to know that the tower steps have been repaired and it is now safe for any of you to take a group of girls up, though obviously all the usual care must be taken and the key returned afterwards to Miss Fairbairn.

The other matter is more serious. You know that it has become a tradition over the past few years for the school to have a blackberry-picking outing this term, each House competing for who picks the most. Regrettably it must be cancelled this year. I have to tell you that there have been several unpleasant incidents in this area. Indeed in other areas too. A prowler entered one school and stole all the silver cups and trophies. In another he found one of the girls and did something much worse. In view of these incidents I do not consider it wise that the girls should spend the day roaming in the lanes in a manner where they cannot be constantly supervised. I think that is all. Unless somebody has anything to raise?"

She allowed her usual very brief pause for the raising of anything, gathered up her papers and left them.

"I can't think what the fuss is about," Helen Rhodes remarked. "It's a rotten year for blackberries anyway."

Miss Pool, who had gone over to the fire and was already frenetically building it up into a black pyramid, looked shocked.

"But she can't take risks with the girls," she said.

"She needn't. She need only have said there wouldn't be an outing because there aren't any blackberries. Which is true."

"Perhaps she wanted to impress upon us..." Puddles' voice trailed off.

"Quite," Helen said as she went out of the room. "I had the feeling that she was trying to impress upon us that something dramatic is about to happen."

Miss Pool shook her head, but was too fearful of appearing critical to put her disagreement into words.

Ruth felt sorry for her, but was inclined to agree with Helen. Mrs Bland's statement had about it a dramatic quality that the Head usually eschewed. But she had other things to think about, three sets of books to mark, mock exam papers to set, tomorrow's lessons to prepare, so she put it out of her mind. Later she remembered.

It was a Saturday evening some two weeks later when the Head sent for her. Such summons were not uncommon; she guessed it would be about the O Level candidates and took the relevant lists with her and the mock exam paper she planned to set them at the end of this term. So she was surprised when Mrs Bland produced sherry and asked her to sit by the fire.

"This is by way of being a celebration," Mrs Bland told her. "Congratulations on the success you are making of your first job."

"Thank you."

She was so astonished that she could think of nothing else to say. It was a good dry sherry too, the sort her father always kept in the house.

"I think you overtaxed yourself at the beginning, but now you are more relaxed. You have natural discipline and I like the way your sixth form classes are more like tutorials than lessons. I presume that is instinctive to you because you come to us immediately from university."

"But how do you know – I mean about the sixth form lessons and–"

"If one happens to take a stroll in the garden and pauses outside the classroom windows, voices can sometimes be surprisingly clear. I have learned a considerable amount in this way, nineteenth century history in your case."

It might have been spooky, this casual eavesdropping, but in Mrs Bland it seemed admirable that she wanted to know as much as she could about her school and her staff.

"I am grateful, my dear," she went on, getting up, which was her way of making clear that the interview was at an end, "not only for what you do here, which is a great deal, but even more for what you are."

She left the Head's study feeling light-hearted for the first time since she came here. It seemed that she had made a success of it, this profession which she had entered so impetuously, without that feeling of vocation which proper teachers are supposed to have. Back in her room the feeling of elation evaporated. There was nobody to tell. She stood in the silence of the empty room, remembering how every success, every small pleasure, even, had been shared with her father. She realised now that much of the pleasure had lain in anticipating the joy he would have in it. They say that a sorrow shared is a sorrow halved, she thought, but the truth is that a joy unshared is a joy halved.

She couldn't stay in here, couldn't settle down to work as if nothing had happened. She would go and tell Michelle. She would be pleased anyway. She ran back downstairs, down the cellar steps and found her way to Michelle's room. The French girl was sitting by the gas fire, nursing a cold.

"You need a drink," Ruth told her. "Listen, I'm celebrating," and she told her briefly what Mrs Bland had said, "so I thought I'd go down and get a bottle of wine," she concluded although the thought had just entered her head. "I can catch the five past seven bus from the bottom of the drive."

"How will you get back?"

"I shall get a taxi," Ruth told her airily. "I've been paid, you know. I'm pretty rich at the moment. Is something wrong, Michelle or is it just your cold?"

"Oh, I am sorry to be bad company. To be true, I'm worried because I have had no letters from home. I was expecting one from my father's friend, the one I told you of. He promised to keep in touch with me if I came here, and he is not a man to break his promise. I have written twice and I should so like a letter from home."

Before she could reply, they heard Esther Fairbairn's voice calling. Michelle went quickly to the door, closing it behind her. But Ruth could hear their voices.

"Please take this box down to the lodge, Michelle. I told Mrs Fox she should have it this evening. Just leave it in the usual place in the porch. There is no need to knock."

"Yes, Miss Fairbairn. I shall go now."

When Michelle came back into the room, they didn't speak for a moment, giving the housekeeper time to get out of earshot.

"I heard all that, Michelle. Why can't she go herself? Can't she see you've got a cold? It's freezing outside."

"I will do everything she asks," Michelle said firmly. "Then I go back to France and never come back – ever."

"But it's such a *shame*. All schools aren't like this. Anywhere else you'd be well treated. I do wish you wouldn't just accept it like some kind of punishment."

Michelle smiled and shook her head.

"You're jolly obstinate," Ruth told her.

"You too would be better elsewhere," Michelle told her. "Yet here you are. Perhaps we are not so different."

Ruth looked at her in surprise. Yes, it was true. It would be so much more sensible to work in some day school in London, living comfortably with her father and Elizabeth. It was just that it was impossible.

"Anyway," she said to change the subject. "You're not going out. I'll take the box and drop it in at the lodge on my way down."

"Thank you very much. You just leave it in the porch. Miss Fairbairn doesn't seem to wish me to get to know the people there."

"She doesn't want you to have any friends at all," Ruth pointed out. "Least of all me."

She glanced at her watch. "Oh lord, I must hurry. I'd better go up and get a coat."

"Take mine," Michelle said, getting out the red coat. "At least we know it fits."

"I promise to take care of it," Ruth said, putting it on. "It's very trusting of you to part with your haute couture effort."

Michelle laughed and handed her the box. Ruth slipped out of the side entrance to avoid Esther Fairbairn and set off down the drive. She went slowly at first, accustoming herself to the dark. The moon was not yet up and there were only a few stars. It was a lovely night, she observed. All the same she knew she would never like having all this dark countryside around her. She wasn't exactly frightened of it; it just made her feel uncomfortable. She only felt at home in towns. Hampstead Heath was the sort of countryside she liked; her father and she had often walked there on a winter evening. True there were trees and grass, but there was always a reassuring hum of traffic in the distance. Sometimes too they drove out to somewhere outside town, in the green belt. What she really liked, she reflected, was countryside that you drove out to and when you'd had enough of it and perhaps it had done you some good, you left it behind and returned home to the town and people and lighted windows. The country was essentially a place you went on an expedition to, not something to have around you all the time. Especially at night.

There was a lamp halfway down the drive. She paused under it to check the time. Her watch showed that it was just ten to seven. She would be in good time for the bus, she thought as she walked away from the pool of friendly light and into the intenser dark.

She had reached the bend where the drive narrowed when something seemed to fall on her from the trees. For a moment she thought it was an animal, then she realized that these were human hands that held her. It was an arm that had her round the shoulders, a human body she was pressed against, a human hand over her mouth. She felt herself lifted up and carried into the bushes.

It was all so sudden that she felt no fear, only surprise. She was aware of the strange sensation of being carried, her feet right off the ground. There was a smoky kind of smell. She felt that she was being carried by an animal to its lair.

She observed it all with a curious detachment. It was all too sudden to make her frightened; there had been no build up of fear, no time for imagination to wreak its havoc.

The hands moved to her neck and at their touch terror flooded her as if released by the moving fingers. She struck out wildly and screamed for help. Instead of a scream only a whispered "help" came out.

For a moment the hands relaxed their hold and by instinct she threw herself away from her captor, making a great bound into the bushes and then running for all she was worth, not trying to regain the path, just get away. He must be just behind her, he would follow her easily she was making such a noise. She imagined sounds behind her, heard breathing. Then she made herself stop and listen. There was no sound other than her own breathing. More quietly and carefully she made her way towards the path, rejoined it near the bottom of the drive and ran towards the road.

She could hardly believe that she had escaped. But there was the road and – almost unbelievably, like some bright rescue ship, – the lighted bus was coming towards her. She flagged it down.

"It's not a stop," the driver grumbled as she got on.

She looked up at him, afraid that if she spoke she would burst into tears.

"Come in, then, m'andsome," he said more kindly.

She sat down, aware that she was trembling. Other passengers looked at her curiously for a moment and then forgot her. The conductor was coming round. She could not speak of what had happened. A few minutes ago she had desperately wanted the help of other human beings, and yet now she felt ashamed in front of all these people going on their evening's outing. She couldn't interrupt their lives with talk of murder. She offered money and received her ticket.

The dark countryside moved past, she stared out at it, seeing danger in every branch of every tree. Only the bus was safe. She wanted never to leave it. It was hard to make herself get out when they reached the town, and even as she walked the few hundred yards through well-lit streets to the police-station she kept glancing fearfully over her shoulder.

She had never been in a police-station before. It looked like an office, except that there was a young policeman at the desk. He looked up and asked what he could do for her.

"I've been attacked," she said.

It sounded absurd; it didn't relate to the panic and the feeling of the fingers at her throat and the terrified running in the dark through the trees.

"Assault, Miss?" the constable said. "That's CID, that is."

He turned away and spoke briefly on the telephone.

"Detective Sergeant Behenna will see you," he said. "Come this way, please."

He led her down a corridor and into a room where a middle-aged man was sitting at a desk writing. He put his pen down as she came in and greeted her wearily. The constable withdrew.

"I understand you allege you have been attacked," Detective Sergeant Behenna said.

"Yes," she said, resenting the alleged. "I *have* been attacked."

"Perhaps you could give me a few details first," he said. "Your name?"

"Ruth Marion Cassell," she said. It sounded strange. What was Professor Cassell's daughter doing in this Cornish police-station telling a strange tale about being attacked in the woods?

"Would you like a glass of water?" the Detective Sergeant asked her patiently. When she said that she would, he had one brought in. She was surprised at how much it hurt her throat to swallow. How tightly the hands must have squeezed. And only a couple of hours ago she was sipping Mrs Bland's sherry without any discomfort at all.

"Now just tell me as briefly and as clearly as you can what happened," the Detective Sergeant said after she had given him details of her home and of her work.

She told him how she had been grabbed from behind and lifted up and carried into the trees.

"May I ask why you didn't call out immediately?" he interrupted. "After all, you were in a school drive. They might have heard cries. Or help might have come from the lodge."

"There was nobody at the lodge."

"Ah, but you didn't know that then. You yourself admitted that you only realized that there was nobody at the lodge when you reached the end of the drive and saw that there were no lights on."

She looked at him in bewilderment, wondering whose side he was on.

"You see, Miss Cassell, it is Saturday night."

"Saturday night?" she repeated stupidly.

"You must realize that we have a great many reports by girls of being attacked, especially on Saturday nights. Most of them, we know from experience, are not genuine."

"But..."

"Please do not think we are accusing you of any falsification."

"Thank you."

"But you will appreciate our dilemma. A girl finds herself in trouble; it's the easiest thing in the world to say she was raped."

"But I *wasn't* raped."

"Oh, I thought you said..."

"I said he grabbed me and I managed to get away. He didn't follow me. I don't know why."

"Ah, well, that's a very different story."

Having established that she was not complaining of being raped, the Sergeant became much more sympathetic. She thought with some dismay of what her predicament would have been if she had.

"Well, we'll take you back to Polglaze now," he said at last when the ordeal by questioning was over. "I'll take some men up with me and we'll have a quick search in the grounds, but I'm not very hopeful of catching your assailant. How do you feel now?"

"Much better, thank you. Except that my throat is sore."

He asked her to pull down the neck of her jumper. The bruises were beginning to show.

"I'm afraid it will mean an examination by the doctor tomorrow," he said. "One needs a medical report as evidence in a cause of assault. But it will be perfectly straightforward."

He led the way out of the room and left her in the outer office while he went to see the other men who were to accompany them. As she sat waiting a man came in to report a lost gold cufflink.

"I've been in town about an hour," he told the young constable at the desk, who was busy entering up the details in a file. "I've been walking about the centre – Cathedral area and so on – so it could be anywhere. I thought I'd pop in and report it, but I don't expect there's much chance of anyone picking it up. But I'd like to have it back. Nice pair," he added, stretching out his wrist to show the one that remained.

She sat, scarcely listening, as the man talked and the young constable took notes.

The Detective Sergeant returned with three other men.

"Right," he said, "I'll take Miss Cassell back with me and the rest of you follow. By the way," he added, turning to the young constable, "I'm up at Polglaze School for an hour if you need me."

The man at the counter turned. "Did I hear you say Polglaze? I'm going up there myself shortly. Can I help? Give the young lady a lift perhaps?"

"Thank you, sir. It's a kind offer, but I'll take her myself."

"Right you are," the man said. Then he turned to Ruth, smiling. He had an agreeable smile.

"You teach there?"

"Yes."

"I go up occasionally to help with the accounts. My name is Eliot. We may meet again."

They shook hands. Then Ruth followed the Detective Sergeant out into the night.

Mrs Bland had both tea and brandy set out in her study ready to offer Ruth. She settled her in an armchair by the fire and saw that she was comfortable, before turning her attention to the Detective Sergeant, who was standing waiting at the far end of the room, through the archway.

"I should be so grateful," Ruth heard her say, "if you could deal with this unfortunate affair with the utmost discretion. It is of course imperative that the girls know nothing of it. The last thing we want is an outbreak of hysteria. Of course, I fully understand that you must do everything possible to find the man and I will co-operate in every way I can."

"Thank you, Mrs Bland. There are just a few things; I gather from Miss Cassell's statement that you already suspected somebody was prowling about?"

"Yes. Our housekeeper thought that she saw a man lurking in the grounds a few weeks ago. Of course, we obviously do have trespassers – with grounds as extensive as ours it couldn't be otherwise. Last summer we even had a party of tourists picnicking on the hockey pitch. But one doesn't want to raise unnecessary alarms. I expect Miss Cassell told you that we had taken the precaution of cancelling our annual blackberrying expedition?"

"That was very wise, if I may say so. You obviously take very seriously your responsibility for these girls."

"And my staff. But I'm afraid I've failed this time," Mrs Bland said.

"Well, we'll do our best to find the man," the Detective Sergeant assured her again. "If you'll excuse me now I'll go and see if the men have anything to report."

After he had gone Mrs Bland pulled her chair up near to Ruth's. "How do you feel now, my dear?" she asked.

"Much better, thank you."

"I'm afraid the marks show," Mrs Bland said, looking at her neck. "Would you mind wearing a scarf? We don't want the girls to notice."

"Yes, I'll do that."

"I can't say how sorry I am," Mrs Bland went on. "Or how responsible I feel for letting this happen."

"It's all right," Ruth said awkwardly. "After what you said at the staff meeting I suppose it was stupid of me to go down there alone at night."

"Well, in future please don't."

"And what about the domestic staff?" Ruth asked. "Miss Fairbairn sent Michelle down there alone."

Mrs Bland's expression hardened. She obviously felt the implied criticism. Then, "I'll speak to Miss Fairbairn in the morning about it," she said. "I can assure you that she is as concerned for the welfare of her staff as I am for mine."

There was no mistaking the note of dismissal in her voice. Ruth got up. "Thank you for the tea and brandy," she said.

She took the coat – Michelle's lovely red coat – from the back of the chair. Mrs Bland followed her to the door and opened it for her.

"Sleep well," she said. "And thank you for being such a brave and sensible person."

Ruth said good-night and climbed slowly up to her room. From the dormitory landing, as she passed, she could hear talking and laughter as the girls went to bed. How strange to think that not very many yards away from all these people she had very nearly been murdered.

She was surprised to find the light on in her room and Michelle sitting waiting.

She jumped up as Ruth came in. "You're so late," she said. "What ever happened? I see no bottle."

Ruth stared at her. She had forgotten the arrangements they had made to meet up here, she had forgotten the original purpose of her trip into town. Everything that had happened before the attack now seemed to belong to the distant past. Worst of all, Michelle didn't even know. She would have to tell it all over again. She walked slowly across the room and sat down wearily on the bed, "I was attacked," she said. "On the way down to the lodge. And Esther Fairbairn's parcel is somewhere in the bushes."

Telling it to Michelle brought it all alive to her. When she had reported it to the police it had seemed like a strange event that had happened to somebody else. Now it was herself, Ruth Cassell, who had almost been murdered. Why me? She found herself saying.

"You will get into bed," Michelle said when she had finished. "And you will drink the warm milk drink I make for you. Then you will sleep and tomorrow you will lie here and I will bring up breakfast on a tray."

She did as she was told, but found herself feeling wide awake.

"You know," she said to Michelle, "I remembered more about it when I told you. I mean I'd forgotten how I stopped under the lamp, for instance. I ought to have told them that – it gave the man a chance to see who I was."

"You mean the man was really trying to kill *you* – not just attacking any woman who came down the drive?"

"I don't know. It's odd though. And it's odd the way he let me get away. I don't know if I explained that properly to the police either. I mean I just know that he could have come after me and got me if he'd wanted. He was very strong and I was making a lot of noise crashing about through the trees."

"Perhaps he was suddenly afraid at all the noise you were making?"

"Yes, I suppose that's possible. But he'd already let me go by then. I really didn't cry out very loud. I meant to, but I couldn't. I suppose it was my throat, or just that I was too scared. But it was then that he let go."

Michelle shivered. "You mustn't go out alone again."

"Or you. Don't you see, it could just as well have been *you*, if you'd gone on Miss Fairbairn's errand?"

"We are lucky, you and I," Michelle remarked.

Ruth laughed aloud. "*Lucky?*" she repeated. "You've got a funny idea of luck."

"We have both had escapes in the last few weeks, me in the tower and you tonight. Though mine, of course, was just an accident."

Ruth nodded. She had decided not to tell Michelle what she had discovered about the light.

"I suppose," she said tentatively, "there couldn't be anyone here who would like to get rid of us both, could there?"

"Tonight you are gloomy," Michelle said. "Why should anybody want to get rid of us? You are useful to Mrs Bland and I to Miss Fairbairn."

"I suppose so. It's odd all the same. By the way, there was a man in the police-station called Eliot. He said he came up here sometimes to do the accounts. Do you know him?"

"Yes, he was up here in the holiday, before you came. And once since I think. But he is mostly with Mrs Bland and Miss Fairbairn you know."

"Yes, I suppose he would be if he's doing the school accounts. He seemed nice."

"We could do with a nice man around the place, to look after us."

Ruth laughed. "You can say that again. Still there's always Albert, he has such a gentle face, hasn't he?"

"He has funny habits."

42

"Such as?"

"He collects any underwear that the girls throw out."

"Oh... Albert."

"You know it is his job to see to all the rubbish and bins and things. Well, if the girls throw any old bras or pants into their waste paper baskets in the dormitories he boards them up. He has a real chestful in his room. It's his hobby."

"Well, I suppose it's harmless," Ruth ~~said~~ nodded and yawned. "Ow, that hurts," she added, stopping in the middle of the yawn.

"Your poor neck! I can't bear to look at the marks."

"Mrs Bland asked me to wear a scarf so the girls won't see."

Michelle's face lit up. "I will make you one," she said, obviously delighted to be able to do something practical. "I have a nice little piece of pink silk and then I can use a piece of the crimson lining left over from the coat to line it with. It will be very pretty."

Ruth laughed. "You're marvellous!" she said. "you and your little bits of material. But the coat – is it all right? It's not torn, is it?"

"No, it won't be," Michelle said, examining it carefully all the same. "Clothes don't tear easily – except in books."

She picked a few bits of twig and a small leaf or two off the coat, shook it, folded it carefully over her arm, said good-night and went back to her room in the cellar.

Ruth lay awake, reliving what had happened, puzzling over the actual attack; the curious way in which a determined effort to kill her had been followed by her sudden release. She didn't fancy the idea of walking down the drive again in the dark. Perhaps she might risk rebuff and ask Helen Rhodes for a lift sometimes in her car. She thought about Helen Rhodes; what was it that she had said after that staff meeting? Something about Mrs Bland preparing the way for something dramatic to happen. Did Mrs Bland know something? She had been at pains to point out the dangers that might lurk in the woods and had obviously been glad that the policemen knew that she had done so. But then one of the endearing things about Mrs Bland was that she was not above such human weakness as liking to be seen to have shown foresight.

All in all, she thought drowsily, just before going to sleep, it might have been much worse. It might have been Michelle, and even if she had escaped it would surely have been the last straw after all the other tribulations she had suffered at Polglaze.

CHAPTER SEVEN

The day that Alastair was coming she did in fact beg a lift from Helen Rhodes. Rather to her surprise the English mistress did not seem to regard it as an assault on her privacy. Once away from the school she was immediately relaxed and friendly.

"It's a damned nuisance," she said as they drove down the long drive, "this Saturday morning school. It breaks up the weekend so. I've done my best to get it cancelled, but I suppose it's too painfully obvious that I am motivated entirely by self-interest."

Ruth laughed. "Yes," she said, "it really is better for the children to have lessons on Saturday morning. The weekends are pretty long in a boarding school; the longer you can delay the start of them the better."

"I don't know how you stand it," Helen remarked. "I couldn't, of course." She had reverted momentarily to the tone of voice which implied that belonging to a different species from the rest of the staff she naturally had different requirements.

"Oh, it's not too bad. They have games in the afternoon. In the evenings we have rehearsals for the play – and on Sundays too."

"Spare me the details," Helen said with some horror.

For a moment Ruth reflected how curious it was that one didn't really mind Helen's rudeness, which seemed to be directed against life rather than oneself. It was a mannerism really, a defence perhaps.

"I hear you've made your garret quite habitable," Helen said. "Miss Pool is all agog about it."

Ruth refrained either from saying that Michelle had helped her or inviting Helen up to see it; silently she reflected how cautious and suspicious she had become in less than half a term at Polglaze.

Helen pulled up by the station. "Here you are," she said. "You're a bit early."

"I don't mind. Thanks for the lift."

"Any time," Helen said. Her expression relaxed a little as she added, "Enjoy yourselves."

She's a nice person, Ruth found herself thinking as she stood on the pavement for a moment watching the car disappear down the road; it's just that she doesn't want anyone to know.

She bought a platform ticket and settled herself to wait on a bench in the sun; it was a pleasantly warm day for late October. But it was no good, she couldn't sit still. She was very excited, she admitted to herself, at the prospect of seeing him again, as she began to pace up and down the platform. When at last the train did come in, he was leaning out of the window, so she saw him first. He didn't see her, so she indulged herself in the pleasure of watching him walking the length of the platform. He was tall so she could see him above the others, looking anxiously for her, his dark hair in need of a cut, flopping about in the wind. Suddenly she couldn't watch him any longer. She ran forward and almost hurtled herself into his arms.

"Oh, but it's good to see you, Ruth, good, good," he repeated, kissing her face again and again. "You're thinner. Are you well? What's this mark on your neck?"

"Nothing, tell you later. Come on."

They were holding up the queue; she caught him by the arm and they made their way out of the station.

"Haven't you any luggage?"

"No, I don't need any. The sleeper gets into London by seven tomorrow morning so I'll go back and shave at the hostel. I didn't want to bring a lot of clutter."

"It's a shame you've got to be back for tomorrow. It's a terrible long way to come for half a day."

"It's worth it," he said glancing down at her.

"We'll make the most of every minute," she promised. "Come on."

He took a deep breath as they came out of the station yard.

"Go on," she said, "tell me how lucky I am to have this lovely country air to breathe instead of London grime."

"You take the words out of my mouth."

"Actually it's the first fine day we've had since I came. Usually it pours with rain and everything drips. If it's warm, it's wet and stuffy with it."

"Unspoilt countryside is absolutely wasted on you," he said, tucking her arm under his as they walked down into town.

"Yes, I suppose I *do* prefer my countryside spoiled. I often think, as I tramp up that drive, that I'd rather be in a street on top of a London bus."

He shook his head, disbelieving.

"But it's true," she insisted. "I splodge along in the mud and I think how much more sensible it would be if *you* were down here and *I* was in London."

"Ah, so you do spare me a thought now and then?" he asked, stopping and looking down on her.

"Come on," she said, "I've been told about a good place for lunch. It' s a bistro with enormous helpings and quite cheap and–"

"All right, I understand; it's not to be discussed. But I do miss you, Ruth, very much." He paused and then resumed more casually. "As you say, it's odd how it's turned out – you, the town girl, working in Cornwall and me, the naturalist, working in London."

"But you like it, don't you? Working in the boys' home, I mean?"

"Oh yes, I love it. It's terribly hard work, of course, we' re so understaffed. I don't think the warden's had a half a day off since I've been there; should be a bit easier because there's another chap coming like me to do a year's practical before going to train."

"And where will you train? London?"

"I'm afraid so. I shall be seconded as a student probation officer and work under somebody qualified. But it's bound to be somewhere where caseloads are heavy. I'd rather do it down here, of course."

"I've told you, we don't have anything down here except trees and rain and outsize slugs – huge black and brown ones and some sickening ones with orange frills."

"Ah *Arion lusitanicus*," he said enviously.

The bistro was in a narrow back street. As he opened the door, he observed that it was small, low-ceilinged and had a pungent smell. It was ill-lit too and that was nice, he thought as he chose a table for them in the darkest corner. The rough walls were covered with Victorian prints and photographs. The little scrubbed deal table at which they sat wobbled slightly on the uneven slate floor. He steadied it by pushing a newspaper under one leg. A wild-eyed young man, wearing a butcher's blue striped apron, came and took their order, returning with two deep bowls of onion soup and a basket of garlic bread.

"You've quite decided about doing social work?" she asked as they ate.

"Yes." He hesitated. "Does it worry you?" he asked.

She laughed. "Goodness, no, why should it? It just seems a waste of all those years of studying the flora and fauna."

"Nothing's ever wasted. Besides, nature study will always be my hobby. But I've thought about it a lot and, when all's said and done, people are more important than plants."

"That's debatable. I should have thought a good environmentalist–"

"Don't niggle, you know what I mean."

"Yes, I know. I agree with you actually."

The wild-eyed young man removed their empty bowls and set before them thick steaks daubed with highly spiced sauce. Then he brought jacket potatoes running with butter and a heaped bowl of salad. He set a carafe of red wine on the table.

They were silent for a while, concentrating. Between them a white candle burnt messily in a wrought iron holder.

"Ruth," he said, filling up her glass. "You said you had half-term in a couple of weeks. Why don't you come up to me in London?"

"I've planned to stay at school and work. You don't know how awful teaching is–"

"Nonsense, you love it. I can see that."

"Yes, I do," she admitted. "It's surprising, isn't it? But what I meant was that it's much harder work that I'd expected. None of the things I did at University are any use to me now. And honestly I just have to prepare every lesson, so I know exactly what I'm going to say – otherwise I'm sunk, and it takes ages."

"All right, I know you'll have to do some work, so why not work all day Friday and then catch the sleeper at night and I'll meet you on Saturday morning at Paddington?"

She hesitated and then said, "I don't really like the thought of going to London, despite all I've said."

"It's because of your father, isn't it?"

"It's no good talking about it. You couldn't understand. I know myself that I'm being stupid. I can't help it."

"Of course, I understand. It's the hardest thing – to share someone you love."

"But I didn't think so. I've always said–"

She broke off.

"I know," he said, reaching across and taking her hand. "Give it time, Ruth. But don't go transferring all your unhappiness to London and keep yourself away from it, because you love the place really, don't you? Besides you have so many friends who want to keep in touch with you–"

"All right. I'll come," she was surprised to hear herself say.

"Good. That's settled. We' ll go straight from here to the station and book you a sleeper before you change your mind. And, by the way, your ticket is your half-term present from me."

"No, I'll pay you back."

"Anything," he told her, learning across the table and taking her hand. "Just so long as you come."

The waiter interrupted them with orange sorbet smothered in Cornish cream.

"We'll need a long walk after this lot," Alastair remarked.

"I thought we might walk up to Polglaze, if you'd like to see my school."

"Of course I would. I want to see everything in your world here."

"We could ask Michelle to come up and have tea in my room, if the old Fairbairn dragon will let her escape."

It was a relief to refer to her in that way. It made her seem less fearsome.

"No," he told her. "We're not inviting anyone to tea. Today is just for the two of us. And I've brought a walletful of money to take us somewhere really special tonight. You choose where."

"Then you'll go straight to the sleeper?"

"Yes, I'll put you safely into a taxi and then catch my train. But let's not think about it. It's hours away."

Later, as they left the bistro, "Do you want to look around the town?" she asked.

"No, I want to go straight back to the station for your ticket."

"Do stop fussing, Alastair. I've told you I've promised to come," she told him, taking his arm as they walked.

"I know, but I'll be happier when it's properly booked."

It was true; he did seem more relaxed once he had handed her the ticket, watched her stow it away in her bag.

"It's quite a long walk," she told him as they set off, "five or six miles."

"Fine by me. You're not tired?"

"No, it's marvellous to be out of the school atmosphere. I hadn't realised how much I'd got bogged down in school affairs. Trivial things become terribly important, you know. I just feel so free now and full of energy."

He smiled down at her, took her hand and they walked briskly up to Polglaze, not talking much, at ease together as they always used to be.

The colours of the trees when they turned into the school grounds were suddenly lit up by the afternoon sun. "What a place to work!" he exclaimed. "Ye gods, you ought to have to pay for the privilege."

"Poor Alastair! It does seem hard. Perhaps one day you'll be able to do probation work in the country."

"I doubt it. The need for probation workers is mostly in the cities. It just shows how bad towns are for people."

It was the old familiar argument; for a moment she nearly told him about the attack in the woods, just to prove that life in the country was every bit as dangerous as in the towns. Then she checked herself; it would be mean to cause him anxiety just to win herself a debating point.

They went in by the side door. Too late she realised that their arrival coincided with that of the children coming in from hockey. They stared at Alastair with uninhibited interest as they swarmed in, swinging their hockey stocks, stamping their feet and shouting at each other. Alastair watched them in alarm.

"Worse than delinquent boys?" she asked him, when they were out of earshot.

"Much more frightening. In fact the whole place terrifies me. What's that smell?"

"I've got used to it. Polish, I think, and gym shoes and girls. The basement is worse – full of coke fumes. Here we are – on my own top landing."

"It's very good as garrets go," he said, when they went into her room.

The room was scarcely recognizable now as the one she had taken over a few weeks ago.

"I was lucky; the little chair and pouffe came from a junk shop. The carpet I got in a sale. It's got a few holes in it but they are mostly hidden under the bed or the table. All the rest of the stuff is Michelle's handiwork. You look around; I'll go and fill the kettle."

When she came back he was looking out of the window.

"It's a pity you've got these bars," he said. "Are they meant to keep you in or others out?"

"Others would have a bit of a climb, wouldn't they?" she said, peering downwards.

"I bet you get a marvellous view from the tower," he remarked suddenly. "I wouldn't mind going up there. Can you get up?"

"No. The dragon has the key."

"We can ask her for it."

She was about to deny this when she suddenly thought there was no reason why they shouldn't. Having Alastair there had emboldened her. The presence of an outsider cut school bullies like the housekeeper down to size.

"All right," she said. "We'll go now. It'll be too dark later. Just wait until the bell goes. Then the girls will be in tea and we shan't meet great hordes of them in the corridors."

Shortly afterwards the bell clanged, there was the surging sound of feet, slamming of doors, shouting, and then silence.

"Right," she said. "It's safe. We'll go and get the key."

They did not need to go as far as the basement. They met Esther Fairbairn as she was going into the Head's private apartments. She would probably have gone on and ignored them, but with her was Mr Eliot who stopped when he saw Ruth. Miss Fairbairn had no choice but to join in the introductions.

"We were wondering," Alastair said, "if we might go up the tower? I should be very interested in looking at the view from up there."

Miss Fairbairn hesitated and then with a sudden ravishing smile she said, "But of course, I'll just run and get the key."

Ruth watched her go with astonishment: certainly the effect on the housekeeper of one young male visitor was wholly beneficial.

"The grounds look enormous," Alastair was saying to Eliot. "How big are they?"

"Twelve and a half acres," Eliot told him.

"I wish we had a fraction of that round our boys' home in London."

"In London it would be worth something – not that land is cheap down here. I heard of a plot the other day going at twenty thousand pounds an acre."

"At that price Polglaze School grounds are worth a quarter of a million pounds," said Alastair, who was always quick with figures.

Eliot did not reply.

"I heard voices," Mrs Bland said, appearing suddenly through the swing doors. "And just had to come to investigate."

Ruth introduced Alastair. They shook hands.

"And how long are you spending here?" Mrs Bland asked him. When he told her their plans, she said, "Well now, why not call in on me for a drink on you way out this evening?"

"We'd like that," Ruth said. "Wouldn't we?" she added, looking up at Alastair whom she sensed would rather have her to himself. However, he seemed genuinely pleased and by the time Miss Fairbairn returned with the key they had arranged to be back in the Head's study at half-past six.

"Be very careful on the tower stairs," Mrs Bland said. "We nearly had an accident up there, remember."

"It's been repaired, Mrs Bland," Ester Fairbairn put in. "It's perfectly safe now."

Detecting the accustomed ferocity in her voice, Ruth quickly said good-bye and led Alastair away in the direction of the tower.

The key turned with surprising ease.

"What was all that about repairs?" Alastair asked. "I'll go first in case it's not safe."

"I'll tell you about the accident later. But I'd like to look at the repair work as we go."

The light was very bright on the spiral stairs; she could imagine how Michelle, who always moved quickly, would have run confidently up without any thought of danger. The treads were wooden; old but quite firm. Fixed with iron rings to the stone wall on the left was a wooden handrail.

Alastair stopped suddenly. "Here are the repair works," he said, pointing to three new wooden treads. The wood was much lighter in colour and stronger than the others. At the side a new section of handrail had been fitted. She examined it all carefully and then told him, very briefly, what had happened to Michelle in the very spot where they were now standing.

"Doesn't it strike you as odd," she said, "that the old wood near the repair isn't in a worse state? It looks to me as if somebody had deliberately cut away the old treads. I mean you wouldn't just get a neat little patch of rot like that, would you?"

"No, but I suppose they would cut it back to the sound wood, wouldn't they? It's been well done."

"I suppose so," she said, rather irked at having her theory dismissed. "Albert is a man of parts."

"Who is Albert?"

"The odd job man. He can pick up trunks as if they were matchboxes. Michelle knows all about him. Apparently he had polio and was for years in a wheelchair but used to haul himself about by his arms, so he is very strong in his top half, shoulders like an ox and all that, but his legs are still very weak, so he can only creep about slowly. But I'm sure he'd be capable of fixing the stairs."

"It's neatly done. I should think Miss Fairbairn got a carpenter in."

"Unless she had her reasons for not getting a stranger in."

"You don't really think she removed the stairs so that Michelle would fall down?"

"I don't know what I think," she said slowly. "I just think that there is something very odd about it, that's all."

"What is rather odd is the way the railing and stairs went in just the same place."

"It's not odd if somebody intended you to lose your foothold and handhold at the same time."

"I suppose it could just be that the rot got into both parts at the same time. Cornwall must be a splendid place for woodworm and rot and all those things."

"So the rot or woodworm simply leapt across the stonework from the stairs to the rail. I don't believe it."

"Let's say the evidence is inconclusive." Then he added, more seriously, "But you don't *really* believe this story about attempted murder, do you?"

She shrugged, not sure what she believed.

At the top of the spiral stairs was a platform from which rose a few stone steps which led out on to the flat roof of the top of the tower. There was a small stone parapet around the edge.

It seemed much higher than she had expected. The evening sun was setting, bringing out the reds and golds of the trees. For miles they could see nothing but the tops of trees.

She breathed deeply. 'I've no idea it would be so lovely," she said.

Alastair was entranced. "It's wonderful to see a proper mixed forest again," he said, "after acres of conifers and afforestation schemes. You could have some lovely walks. I'd rather think of you safely down there in the woods than up this rickety old tower."

Again she almost told him how safe the woods had proved to be, but again stopped herself.

"Yes, it's a naturalist's paradise," she said instead. "Wasted on me."

"It's as good a place as any to propose in," he said. "Do you think: you might ever bring yourself to marry me? Oh, Ruth, I've missed you so much – every day since you went away, I've missed you."

It was what she'd always dreaded. She liked him too much to bear the thought of hurting him.

"I'm sorry. It's still no." Then because she thought he deserved an explanation, and it had to be an honest one, she went on, "You see, I haven't missed you like that. I mean I would have done, wouldn't I, if I'd loved you enough to get married? And I'd be sure, the way you are sure, wouldn't I? I'm so sorry."

"Don't be sorry," he said lightly. "It's the nearest you've ever come to saying 'Yes'."

The sun disappeared behind the trees, the air was cold and raw.

"Come on," she said. "Let's go down."

"You ought to have a tray under that gas ring," he said later as they sat in her room having tea. "Or you'd burn the whole school down."

"I sometimes think it would be a good thing if somebody did," she remarked, watching him lift the ring, complete with the kettle, on to the green tiles of the hearth.

"You sound if there are a few people you wouldn't bother to remove from the blaze."

"Well, yes, there's Esther Fairbairn for a start. Then there's a girl called Sandra Forbes in the Upper IV that I'd be happy to be without."

"What's wrong with Miss Fairbairn that she gets put on the cremation list? I mean apart from the suspicion that she might have been hacking holes in the tower steps?"

That was the trouble; it did seem so unlikely sitting here by the gas fire eating buttered crumpets. It hadn't seemed so when Michelle had told her in her wretched room in the cellar the night it happened.

"Even apart from that, everything's wrong with her, Alastair. She's an insidious influence, and she creeps about the place in soft shoes and she prevents anybody getting to know Mrs Bland, and she treats poor Michelle like a drudge and is generally horrible."

She was aware of sounding silly and petulant. An awareness which was borne out by his saying, "Well, you get these situations in all communities; I expect a girls' school is bound to have its share of oddities. Then everything gets so intense and magnified because you're all cooped up here miles away from anything."

"That's a change from your usual line about lovely mother nature lying all unspoiled around us," she said shortly, irked by the way he dismissed fears which back in school, now seemed to her perfectly rational.

He put down his cup. "I know you're worried," he said. "Tell me exactly what happened. I haven't had the whole story yet."

When she had finished he said, "It's very odd about the lights, certainly. Though I suppose anybody going down the corridor could have switched it off."

"The children were all in tea and anyway that corridor leads nowhere except to the tower."

"Or the bulb could have failed – a nice piece of timing, I admit. And be replaced by now."

"Ye-es."

"You don't want to be convinced, do you?"

"That's not fair; of course I want to be convinced that Michelle isn't in danger. If this wasn't an accident then somebody is going to have another go at her, aren't they?"

"Yes. I'm sorry. But I think you have to be sure that you're not just indulging in a pretty strong dislike of the housekeeper woman."

"It was jolly odd the way she immediately pointed out that it was all Michelle's fault and she hadn't understood and so on. If that didn't point to guilt I don't know what does."

"But she *would* feel guilty anyway if one of her staff nearly had a fatal accident. It's quite normal human cowardice to react by blaming the girl. It doesn't make her a murderess."

"No. I suppose not."

"You never told me about the mark on your neck," he said, thinking he was changing the subject.

She hesitated. Then she told him. If he had seemed to dismiss the story of Michelle's incident too lightly, he was horrified by what had happened to Ruth.

"But it was only a chance thing – it could have happened to anybody," she said.

"But it didn't happen to just anyone," he pointed out, putting his arms around her, enfolding her as if to bestow some retrospective protection. "My God, I'd like to get you away from this place."

She laughed. "What, away from the lovely safe countryside? Back to dangerous London?"

"Don't laugh about it. How can you? When you think that in a few minutes you might..." his voice petered out and he clung to her wordlessly.

"But I got away. It's not the sort of thing that happens twice in a lifetime. I've had my turn. I'm probably safer than most people now."

"My God, you're so calm about it!"

"I wasn't at the time. But remember I've had quite a while to get used to the idea. I wish I hadn't told you now. It's too late to help and you'll only worry."

"You'll be careful, won't you? You'll never go down there alone again?"

"Promise. If you'll promise to forget it."

"I'll try," he said.

And for a while they did forget it as they lay entwined together on Michelle's rag mat in front of the spluttering gas fire.

"I don't feel as if I'm in Polglaze School at all," she said. "I feel as if I'm back in your digs, by your gas fire and still a student..." She stopped on the verge of saying something about still having a father.

"Yes, it was always good there, wasn't it? It wasn't so good when we went to your home though."

He had never referred to it before, to the way that something about being with her father, even being in his house, had undermined him, put some kind of obstacle between him and her so that nothing flowed between them, just a divide. She ached at the memory of it. She understood so much better now, was able to see the situation for what it was. Poor Alastair, somehow excluded by the close bond between her father and herself. It should not have been like that.

It was nearly time to go.

"I'll clear up the wreckage," he said, "while you get ready."

As she gathered up her clothes to go and have a bath, she watched him picking his way among the debris on the floor, big feet placed carefully between jars of honey and packets of butter, making a neat pile of plates and saucers. He was much more methodical than she was.

"Don't be too long," he said as he opened the door for her. He spoke anxiously as if some fell danger awaited her in the bathroom.

She laughed and then clung to him. Tomorrow she would be alone again in this institution, not quite her whole self anymore, she thought as she tipped her face back to be kissed.

"When you twist your head up like that," he said softly, "with your eyes shut and your lips apart, you look so sweet – like a baby bird waiting to be fed."

"God, it's a terrible thing to have a naturalist manqué for a lover," she said pushing him away, but so gently that the gesture seemed to him to be almost as promising as an embrace.

She lay in the bath wishing he could stay longer; if only he didn't have to leave so soon. Because perhaps I do love him really. When I wouldn't tell him my address it was because I was numbed by the thought of Elizabeth and – the marriage. She still shied away from naming her father in the same breath as Elizabeth, from placing them so close together even in her mind. I just wanted to get away from everything and everybody in the old life.

It wasn't true that she hadn't missed him; she shouldn't have said that in the tower. It was just that since she came here she had been overwhelmed by the amount of work there was to do; the children lived so much in the present, filling her time with innumerable small, essential things to be seen to, apart from the ceaseless pressure of teaching all day and marking and preparing half the night. She had neither the time nor the energy to spare for Alastair; she had been utterly taken up with what Helen Rhodes had called the fight for survival. But all the time she hadn't really forgotten him and when she saw him at the station – she felt again that sudden unexpected rush of joy.

She'd been a fool. She did love him really, yes enough to marry him. She imagined how he would look when she told him, the joy on his face. She lay in the bath revelling in the end of uncertainty.

The only decision now was when she should tell him. Certainly not here in Polglaze School. She would wait until they went out this evening. After having a drink with Mrs Bland they were going to get a taxi into the town. No, she wouldn't tell him in the taxi; country taxis lacked the privacy of proper London cabs. Besides she wanted to see his face when she told him. She would wait until they were in the restaurant and the meal ordered. The restaurant would be the *Parakeet*. She'd heard about the restaurant, owned by an Italian, but had never been inside, just glimpsed the little dining room through the curtained windows. Mrs Hamilton-Smythe had once remarked that it was a ridiculous place which had candles on the tables even though the war was over. Any place that Mrs Hamilton-Smythe disliked must be good, she thought, imagining how it would be. With the first glass of wine, when he looked across the table and raised his glass to her, as he always did, she would tell him. She savoured the moment, picturing the scene: she would make it as special and romantic as possible, to atone for all her previous refusals, hedging, postponements. How patient he had been with her, she thought, remembering with shame that she had not always been particularly kind. She had been spoilt, she realised suddenly. Her father had spoiled her. Not only her father, everybody had always spoiled her. She had never been at the receiving end of unkindness until she came to Polglaze School.

When they went to Mrs Bland's room, Eliot was already there. Miss Fairbairn, to Ruth's relief, was too busy seeing to the preparation of the girls' supper. She had actually apologized quite warmly and politely for this when they returned the key of the tower. Ruth began to feel that she had misjudged her and she could see that Alastair thought so too.

"This room is always several degrees too hot for me," Eliot said as they went in. "Let me take your coat."

Alastair, who was wearing a thick wool-lined jacket, removed it gratefully and Eliot hung it up outside in the hall.

Both he and Mrs Bland were welcoming, slightly parental towards the younger couple. Ruth wondered if perhaps they guessed. The room was warm and conversation very easy.

Mrs Bland revealed a surprising knowledge of natural history; she and Alastair were soon deep in conversation. At the far end of the room, under the archway, she had a bookcase full of books on Cornwall. The two of them wandered up to the other end of the room together. Ruth and Eliot stayed by the fire.

Eliot was a formidably charming man, she thought, at first slightly distrustful of his conventional good looks, his poise. His eyes, she told herself, behind the charm, were hard. She couldn't imagine a situation in which he would not be completely in control. But alcohol and the warmth of the fire, and the relaxed and easy way he talked soon melted her distrust. He was very amusing too. More than that. He was really funny.

"There's a lot of laughter going on back here," Mrs Bland remarked returning with Alastair, both of them holding books.

"By the way, how are you young things proposing to get to town tonight? Presumably you're not going to walk in those glamorous clothes?"

"We wondered if we might use the phone to ring for a taxi?" Alastair asked. "We should have done it earlier really."

"Nonsense," Eliot said. "I'm going down myself, and I'll be delighted to take you."

Alastair hesitated; Ruth could see that he hated to be beholden to the older man.

Memories of the strain that beset Alastair in the presence of her father flooded in on her.

"It's quite all right," she said, "thank you – it won't take a minute to ring."

"Nonsense," Eliot said dismissively. "It's absolute nonsense to subsidise the taxi service. And really I'm not just saying it. I am going to town for a bite, myself."

"You know you're welcome to stay at school for a meal, Mr Eliot," Mrs Bland put in.

He laughed. "I've been asked already," he said, "and as you know I have a high regard for the way Miss Fairbairn organises the cooking, but what I can't face is the procession into the dining room. No, thanks very much, I'll be off for a meal on my own."

"Then we'd be grateful for a lift," Alastair said, to Ruth's relief. It really would have been too childish to insist upon getting a taxi to come all the way up here, just in order to drive down behind Eliot's car.

"I'll get the coats," Eliot said. He went out.

"Bless you both, my dears," Mrs Bland said. "Have a lovely evening."

"Thank you so much," Alastair said, shaking her warmly by the hand. "Next time I come, I'll take Ruth for a walk to the place which has those spotted orchids."

"Meanwhile, I'll try and educate her a bit," Mrs Bland said. "For an educated girl she has some astonishing lacunae in her knowledge of the flora and fauna around her."

"It's being short-sighted," Ruth said. "That's my excuse and I'm sticking to it. I just don't *see* the spotted bugloss and the double breasted seersucker."

They laughed and Eliot returned with the coats. They said goodnight again to Mrs Bland and went out to the car.

Ruth was going to get in the front, but Eliot insisted that she and Alastair sat together in the back. "I'm the chauffeur tonight," he said firmly. She took Alastair's hand, trying to convey to him that just showed what a nice chap Eliot was and he needn't be so very distrustful of him.

So they were together in the back of the car when, halfway to town, Alastair said, "It's gone. My wallet's gone. It was in my coat pocket."

At first they could hardly believe it. He went through all his other pockets. "Well, at least my train ticket is safe," he remarked, taking it from his trouser pocket. "I didn't put it back in my wallet after I got off the train."

"When did you last actually see it?" Ruth asked in a whisper.

"I remember having it at the station when we booked your sleeper."

"What did it have in it?"

"All my money and my cheque book."

The extent of the calamity silenced her.

"And I haven't brought any money at all," she said. "I've got a bit back at school, but not enough to go out on tonight, anyway."

They were talking in whispers.

"We'll let him drop us off, then we'll take a taxi back to school, get what you've got and have a cheap meal somewhere."

"It'll be awful if we meet Mrs Bland though, and honestly I don't think your wallet is up there. You tidied everything up – I'm sure we'd have seen it."

"Is there trouble in the back?" Eliot asked. "There seems to be some frantic arguing going on."

Neither of them spoke. But his voice was so warm and friendly she knew it was absurd not to confide in him. She squeezed Alastair's hand.

"We've had a calamity," she said lightly. "Alastair's wallet has vanished."

"I most likely left it at the station," Alastair said. "I'd be very grateful if you could drop us off there and I'll enquire. They're sure to have it in the office."

"By all means," Eliot said and the concern in his voice was unmistakable. "We'll go straight there now. They're always very good at keeping things for you. I dropped one at Paddington myself a few years ago and felt pretty unhopeful about it. But they had it at the office and seemed to think it was quite a routine matter. People leave them at the booking office when they're getting their tickets. It'll be safe enough. Don't you worry."

Eliot kept on chatting. His passengers tried not to think about what they would do if the wallet wasn't at the station.

It wasn't.

Alastair came back, dejected, to the car where Eliot and Ruth were waiting.

"Hop in," Eliot said. "Look, I'd be delighted if you'd be my guests at the *Parakeet*. It's a nice little place, run by an Italian I've got to know a bit. Interesting chap, prisoner of war, but he decided not to go back afterwards, brought his family over and started this little restaurant, pretty brave thing to do with rationing still going on until a couple of years ago. But they're good at managing, these Italians, his wife's a cook and the kids help out, grow their own vegetables, keep hens. It's a cosy little place. I think you'll like it."

"I was going to choose the *Parakeet*," Ruth remarked, surprised.

"Well, there's not a lot of choice, is there? So we'll have a meal there and then you two can go off and amuse yourselves until it's time for the sleeper."

"We can't accept. Thanks all the same," Alastair told him, sounding Ruth thought, shrill and unfriendly.

"Well, if you'd rather," Eliot told him, "just let me lend you some money and I'll drop you off at the restaurant."

He offered so kindly, but it was awful to imply that they'd take his money, but not his company, for a meal.

"Well, my offer stands," he said. "You young things decide what you'd prefer and I'll fit in with your plans."

It went through Ruth's mind that what they'd really like would be for him to drive them back to school so they could hunt for the wallet, but she knew that they couldn't possible ask for such a thing. In the end they said they would accept his kind offer of going out together for a meal.

Alastair did it will ill grace, she noticed with embarrassment, and insisted that he should repay the money later.

"As you wish," Eliot said lightly. "You can foot the lot if you insist. Anything to make you feel happier."

He was fun, she thought, so easy. It was ridiculous to fuss on when Eliot was obviously so much richer than either of them. Alastair was behaving like a grumpy adolescent, with a tolerant and long-suffering father. To compensate she was extra polite to Eliot.

It could have been a marvellous evening; the restaurant was welcoming and simple, softly lit by candles stuck into Chianti bottles, the tables spread with cheerful red and white checked cloths. The food was superb and Eliot was generous. But Alastair was difficult from the start. He refused a drink when they were ordering the meal and Ruth knew it was just because he wouldn't be able to pay for one in return.

Eliot was tolerant, making a joke of it. "Look here," he said, "we'll have a system. I'll count up round two and put it on your bill. But you see I want another drink, even if you don't. I don't know about Ruth?"

She hesitated.

"There's a long wait ahead," he said. "Those lasagne take them a long time to make. They have to beat out the pasta and hang it on the trees to dry. You'd be amazed at the capers they get up to, wouldn't she, Carlo?" he asked the proprietor who was standing by ready to take their orders.

In the end they all three had another drink before going in to the meal.

It set the pattern for the evening. Her respect for Eliot increased at every encounter. He was so patient and kindly; he couldn't have been more tolerant. Alastair was quiet and somehow watchful. When they raised their first glass of wine she thought *this was the moment when I was going to tell him.* Her eyes unaccountably filled with tears.

The meal went on for so long that there was no time left for her and Alastair to spend alone together before the train was due. So they all went together to the station, but once again, Eliot was charming and tactful; he parked outside the station, said goodbye to Alastair, assured them both that it would be a pleasure for him to wait and then drive Ruth safely back to school.

They walked in silence into the station yard.

"I'll see you off," she said. "Do you know I've never seen a sleeper before?"

"There's no need," he said. "You don't want to keep Eliot waiting."

She turned on him angrily. "For goodness' sake, what's got into you? You've behaved like a spoilt child all evening!"

They were walking along the platform towards the bridge.

"I just didn't like taking everything from him," Alastair said miserably. "It wasn't the sort of evening I'd planned."

They were climbing the steps and her voice came out erratically, sounding more accusing than she had intended.

"That was because you lost your wallet. It wasn't Eliot's fault. He was just helping out. And it's so stupid to spoil a whole evening by fussing over who pays."

They were at the top of the steps now. Their footsteps echoed hollowly as they walked across the bridge.

"It wasn't a question of *money*. Surely you could see that it was something other than that?"

"No. My understanding is rather limited when it comes to sympathising with your bad manners."

She walked down the stairs with little angry steps, aware of being slightly drunk.

"Oh, Ruth," he said, as they reached the platform where the train was just arriving, "I've ruined everything."

She was shocked by the despair in his voice, it seemed to go right through her. She was turning to him, ready to hug the hurt away, to tell him she understood, that we all act stupidly when are hopes are dashed, that she loved him, when an attendant jumped down from the train and asked,

"Both travelling?"

"No, just me," Alastair said.

"This way then, Sir," the attendant said, taking him over so that she never got a chance to talk to him alone again.

She watched miserably as the train went out. I'll write, she thought. I'll write and tell him that I'm coming just the same.

It warmed her to think that she too would be catching the same sleeper in a fortnight's time.

She kept watch until the train was out of sight, then she turned and walked out of the station to where Eliot was waiting for her in the car.

CHAPTER EIGHT

Eliot behaved impeccably. When she got back to the car she was feeling confused and apprehensive and even wondering if she ought to apologise for Alastair's behaviour, but he made it quite unnecessary by saying, as he opened the passenger door for her, "What a nice chap. I like 'em independent like that."

At these reassuring words, she settled herself back in her seat and relaxed. It was very pleasant to feel that she was being looked after, that all she had to do was sit and feel drowsy and not even bother to talk, just watch the dark countryside slip by.

How awful it would be, she thought as they turned up the drive to school, if he made a pass at her, but she need not have feared. He continued kind and protective: at school he opened the front door for her, saw her safely inside and closed the door behind her.

The days passed quickly after Alastair's visit. Lessons went well and in the staff room too the atmosphere improved, probably because Esther Fairbairn was hardly ever there. She seemed to have withdrawn to the basement or to the Head's private apartments. Without her, the others were more welcoming and friendly, so she took to going in much more for tea and coffee, even to working there in the evening by the fire, rather than in her own room. Perhaps this was why she saw less of Michelle, or perhaps the French girl was being kept busier downstairs. Either way she scarcely saw her all that week.

She did see more of Eliot, however. She was walking up from town one afternoon, when a car drew up and Eliot called out, "You're laden. In you get and I'll take you up to school."

He put the library books and shopping on the back seat, while she climbed obediently into the front.

"I go into town most Wednesday afternoons," she explained. "The children have games and it gives me a free double period. Sometimes I catch the bus back, but I missed it today."

"You know," Eliot said. "It would be worth your while to get a car. Do you drive?"

"Yes, my father taught me, and I have passed my test – second go. But I haven't had any practice since. I can't afford a car anyway."

"You ought to keep your driving up all the same."

"Ye-es, I suppose that if I stayed down here it might be worth it..."

"Look here," Eliot said. "Why not let me take you out for a practice sometimes? Have you got a licence?"

"Yes, but would you really let me drive this car? Don't you mind?"

"I'd be delighted. So long as you have a current licence, and wear your glasses," he added with mock severity. He had teased her before about not wearing them out of vanity.

"Yes," she said humbly, "I'll do that. I promise."

"Meanwhile," Eliot went on, "I'll keep a look out for a little second-hand car, if you like. You'd find it very useful, you know."

"Yes, though I don't get out much. Just sometimes I miss it. Michelle and I wanted to go to a film a couple of weeks ago, but we couldn't because the only night we were both free the buses didn't fit in and it was absolutely pouring. It would have been very handy to have had a car to jump into."

"You should have asked me. What was the film?"

"You'll laugh. It was *The Prime of Miss Jean Brodie*; just the thing for a schoolmarm having a night out, don't you think?"

"It's probably still around, in the area. They do the rounds you know; Newquay, Truro, Falmouth. I'll look it up in the *West Briton* and let you know."

She thanked him and got out of the car. As he followed her into the school, she asked him if he would come up to her room for tea.

"No, thanks," he said, after a moment's hesitation. "I'd love it really but I can't run the gauntlet of all those kids."

She laughed. "They're in tea themselves, but just as you like."

Again he hesitated. "Well, if I'm honest," he said, "it's partly that I don't want to cause *you* any embarrassment."

She was touched by his solicitude; he was a marvellously considerate and thoughtful man. There was something agreeably old-fashioned and honourable about the way he protected her.

"Alastair came up," she pointed out.

"Oh, that's different – boyfriends of your own age. I'm old enough to be your father and – well, let's just leave it at that. I'd hate to do anything to compromise you in any way."

He paused then added, "I've grown far too fond of you for that."

He smiled; he had a wonderful smile, warm and somehow comforting and yet a little sad; it made her want to show him how grateful she was for all his kindness, his undemanding, fatherly kindness. Eliot: even his name had the strength of an institution. It was both his Christian name and his surname, although he did have another name, which he didn't like and would not tell her. He liked her to call him Eliot, so of course she did.

After he had gone, she dumped the books in her room and went to find Michelle. She found her in the basement, about to carry crates of milk up to the servery. Ruth was shocked at the sight of her; Michelle's face was drawn and pinched, and she looked ill.

"I just came to see if you'd come and have coffee up in my room, Michelle. After supper, I mean."

"Yes, please, I'll come when I'm free," Michelle said, her face lighting up at the invitation.

Guilt-stricken that such a small act could seem so important to her neglected friend, Ruth couldn't stop making excuses: "I'm so sorry I haven't seen you for ages. We've been awfully busy and –"

"I understand," Michelle interrupted. "You have so many duties. But I will come up tonight. Excuse me now for it is nearly teatime."

She offered to help with the crates, but Michelle refused to let her and, fearing to bring down Miss Fairbairn's displeasure on both their heads, Ruth left her to struggle alone.

"Have you heard from home yet?" she asked Michelle as they sat by the gas fire.

Michelle shook her head. "I cannot understand it," she said. "I have written three times and still get no reply."

"Oh, Michelle, I am sorry. I can see you're worried sick. Can't you ring him up?"

"I have thought of it. I could go into the town, but you see you have to book a call and be rung back and it would be very difficult."

"But why not from school? There's a phone downstairs."

"And everything I say heard by Miss Fairbairn? I dare not."

Ruth looked at her, surprised at the fear and dislike in her voice. She had almost forgotten her own feelings for Esther Fairbairn not so very long ago.

"How are things down there?"

"Awful," Michelle said simply. "She is watching me all the time. I am sure she knows even now that I'm up here. I never see my aunt..."

"If I were you I'd go to Mrs Bland and tell her all about it, how you haven't heard from home – everything."

"Sometimes I feel like it; forgive me, tonight is a bad night. But I won't do it. I don't want to give in. It is not very long now. Soon will be half term which is so late that we are much more than halfway through."

"Have you made any more clothes?" Ruth asked to change the conversation. "I'll model for you again."

Michelle shook her head.

"Look, you get yourself some material and make yourself a dress. It was fun doing the coat. It gets you up here in the evening, and it's company for both of us. If I'm busy working you can still sew up here. It doesn't disturb me."

"Yes, I will," Michelle said with sudden resolve. "I will make myself be more jolly."

Ruth laughed. "I like that," she said, "you mean you'll snap out of it?"

They talked and laughed and Michelle, she thought, seemed more her old self by the time she left. All the same she was relieved to notice, when she happened to meet the postman in the drive the following afternoon, that among the letters was one from France. She hadn't time to turn it over and see if it was addressed to Michelle before Mrs Bland appeared and took them from her. But the address on the back showed that it was from Paris, so it seemed likely to be for Michelle. She rejoiced for her friend.

It was very typical of Eliot, she though, to include Michelle in the invitation to go to Falmouth to see the film. She was glad that he did. She was glad too that Michelle refused.

After the film they walked along the narrow winter streets of the deserted town to a restaurant overlooking the harbour. By their table was a porthole window through which she could see the lights of the boats reflected on the water. During the gaps in the conversation she could just hear the distant clattering of the masts as the rigging moved in the evening breeze.

It was natural after such a film that they should talk of schools.

"Tell me," Eliot said. "How do you find life at Polglaze? I mean the atmosphere must get a bit fraught sometimes, doesn't it? All you women cooped up together."

She laughed. "But the awful thing is," she said, "that you don't realise it until you get out, like this."

"Then you should get out like this more often," Eliot said. He spoke with meaning. There was silence. Then he said more lightly, "You know I always feel perfectly safe in Private House, but once through those swing doors among the kids and I'm terrified."

She laughed. "You get used to it," she said. "At first I felt terribly isolated among all those children. And conspicuous too. It was as if I ought to be in uniform as well."

"God forbid."

"But you know you get so involved in detail, so concerned about the individual that you don't see it as an outsider any more. When a horde of about a hundred children surges out of the dining room at me now, I just think Oh Lord, there's Penelope Whatsit and I haven't marked her prep yet."

He laughed. "I met a chap I knew at school a while ago, and he is some kind of eye doctor. We were talking about transplanting retinas, and I said it must be jolly spooky to go into a morgue and start removing eyeballs from dead bodies. He was quite surprised and said not in the least: he was so absorbed with the minutiae of the operation that he never stopped to think about the rest of it."

"What a grisly comparison!" she said. "Anyway, how do *you* come to be involved at Polglaze?"

He hesitated. "Through Miss Fairbairn," he said. "Actually, we are distantly related."

"Oh, I'd no idea."

"It's all right," he said, touching her hand briefly as if to reassure her. "I know you don't like her; I suppose that's why I didn't mention it. I didn't want the dislike to spread to me."

"Oh, it wouldn't. I mean, I don't dislike her, why should I? I've no reason to. I hardly know her."

"Don't be embarrassed," he said. "I didn't mean you in particular. I just meant she's not an easy person to like – except by a few favourites. And you wouldn't be one of those."

She didn't know how to take this, so she sipped her wine and looked out at the lights that trembled on the water and listened to the distant clatter of rigging.

"She's had a hard life, Esther Fairbairn," Eliot said thoughtfully.

"Yes, I gathered that from something she once said to me," Ruth said, remembering her first awful day at Polglaze.

"She's a very capable person. She was brilliant at school but never had a chance to develop her mind. It was all there – thwarted. No wonder she became bitter. She had a younger brother and everything went on him. And he wasn't worth it. But he was the one who was sent to University – and wasted every minute."

"It sounds so Victorian!"

"Well, it was in a way. There have been changes, you know, even between Esther Fairbairn's schooldays and yours. Besides, her family was Victorian. Her parents married late – I should think her mother must have been forty by the time Esther was born. Her father was a hard man – a rector in a Parish up North. She idolised him but in reality he never stood up for her and when her mother died, he took it for granted that she would stay at home and be his unpaid housekeeper. He said it was a girl's duty: selfish old devil. So when he died she was left homeless and untrained. Her brother turned out a wastrel– who sponges on her still."

"Poor thing, no wonder she's so bitter," Ruth said thinking what a wonderfully understanding man Eliot was; he had spoken with such feelings, as if he could really put himself in the place of that rector's daughter, suffer her frustration.

"Oh, she's bitter all right." Eliot said. "And both she and her brother have inherited their father's uncontrollable temper. God help anyone who hurts *their* pride. The Fairbanks are a murderous lot when roused."

"But you know," Ruth said. "I should have thought there'd be plenty of jobs for people like Miss Fairbairn. She's very capable, as you say, and a marvellous organiser–"

"There should be, but nowadays you get nowhere without your bit of paper and she has no qualifications of any kind. She knows her worth and yet sees herself as being fit for nothing but domestic work."

"But there *are* courses, training schemes–"

"Oh Ruth," he said, shaking his head. "You speak with the voice of your generation. But you see the Esther Fairbairns of this life don't – can't – see it that way. Grants, courses; can you see her retraining alongside young students? She despises the lot of them! She's a martyr if you like – certainly there's an outsize chip on her shoulder."

She felt like a child corrected. Yet not made to feel ashamed of her lack of understanding.

"In a way," he said, "the worst thing was that she accepted that selfish old man's belief that it was her duty as a daughter to give up her life to looking after him. Without that she might have been a very successful career woman; I think such a life would have satisfied her. But as it is–" he shrugged. "And then she met Mrs Bland," he said, "and her fate was sealed."

She looked up, expecting him to go on, but he said, "Well, let's not spoil the evening talking shop," and she realised that he had recollected that it was her employer that he had referred to and was, quite rightly changing the subject. Not for the first time she wished that Eliot did not have quite such high standards. A bit of gossip about Mrs Bland would certainly not have spoiled her evening.

The car was difficult to start; it stalled several times on their way back to school.

"There was nothing wrong until it went in for servicing yesterday," Eliot grumbled.

"I expect they've filled it up with the wrong mixture."

As he turned up the school drive, it stalled again.

"Would you mind very much," he asked, "if I left the car here and we walked up?" I really shall have problems if I get stuck halfway up that muddy lane. From here I can run it downhill."

"I don't mind," she said, opening the door. "It's a lovely night. In fact if you're worried, I can easily go up by myself."

"Alone? Indeed you can't! What would your Young Lochinvar have to say?"

She laughed – it was rather a nice description of Alastair. He always looked ready to ride alone and unarmed against all comers. She felt guilty at laughing at him, as she had done when her father made similar remarks.

"All right," she said quickly. "Anyway, if I'm honest, I'm scared stiff of walking up here."

"Poor Ruth," he said, putting his arm around her shoulder. She pictured his big hand – he had big, well-shaped hands – against the dark stuff of her coat. She could feel his hand against her neck.

The walked together until they reached the corner where she had been attacked.

"What are you doing at half term?" he asked suddenly. "You'll go home I suppose?"

"I don't know. I haven't quite decided."

"Your family is in London?"

"My father is. My mother died when I was five."

She hesitated, horrified to find an unswallowable lump had arisen in her throat. She said as firmly as she could, "He got married again last summer."

It didn't come out as the matter-of-fact statement she had intended. It came out as a kind of subdued howl.

"That's the trouble, isn't it?" he said gently. "Why don't you tell me about it?"

She hesitated. She knew she wouldn't be able to tell him calmly; it would be better to go on keeping silent. But the need to speak was now compelling; she couldn't stop. She told Eliot about her father and how they had lived together, about the home they had made, about the almost absurd way he had done everything so thoroughly, so lovingly, all the tasks that did not come easily to him. She told him about it all, even the fitted dressing table and the white carpet. She shouldn't have spoken of it, she realised as she broke down, it was unspeakable, unbearable that her father had broken trust with her.

"Cry, my dear. You need to cry," Eliot said and, obediently, she leant against him and sobbed in his arms.

He didn't speak, except to murmur endearments as he caressed her hair and neck with his big, gentle hands. In the distance a car blew its horn and, as if prompted by the need to ensure her privacy, he drew her gently off the path and into the dark cover of the trees.

CHAPTER NINE

To say that Michelle chose her material with care would be an understatement. She chose it with fanaticism. She felt every roll of cloth, gently tugging at it, holding it up against the light, wrapping it around her. As a sculptor chooses the piece of marble that he knows contains the statue his skill will reveal, so Michelle chose the stuff out of which her dress would finally emerge. She left the fabric department in chaos and the assistants exhausted, but she was blissfully unaware of this as she walked back to school clutching the raw material of her art.

"It's pretty, is it not?" she asked Ruth that evening as she spread out the pale grey material. "It will look well under the red coat?"

"It's gorgeous. But I'm not going to watch while you hack. It scares me stiff."

She concentrated on making coffee while Michelle, without benefit of pattern, cut the material up with complete confidence.

"I don't know how you dare," Ruth remarked as they sat by the fire afterwards. "Just think of the waste if you made one false snip."

Michelle laughed. "But it's easy," she said. "I think it all out in my head and then, snip, I cut to match my idea."

"It takes courage, all the same," Ruth said. "You are a brave kind of person."

"Not when it is a matter of Esther Fairbairn," Michelle said.

Ruth glanced at her: Michelle's present fears – like her own in the past – now seemed to her absurdly exaggerated. There was nothing of the potential murderess about Miss Fairbairn, just rather a pathetic spinster approaching middle age, who had been deprived of a chance to made a career for herself. No wonder she was angry with life!

"Anyway," she said, "you'll be feeling happier now that you've had a letter from home."

"But I have had no letter," Michelle said in surprise.

"Oh, I am sorry. I shouldn't have said anything. But I thought I saw one for you when I handed the post in the other day. I just saw the back and it was from France, so I assumed it was for you – it was stupid of me."

"How did you know it was from France?"

"Well, you know how you always write the name of the sender on the back? This one said Exp: then something or other, Paris, France."

"Ruth," Michelle said urgently. "Please try to remember. Can you think what was the address or the name?"

She thought hard, trying to see again the sloping writing, the royal blue ink on pale blue paper. "It was Philippe," she almost shouted as she suddenly remembers. "And then something beginning with a G. It was a funny name with an apostrophe in the middle. It's no good. I can't remember."

Michelle had gone quite pale. In a whisper she said, "I knew it. They are stealing my letters. The name of my father's friend is Philippe Guyomarc'h. It is a Breton name, although he is Parisian."

Ruth lay awake for a long time that night wondering if she ought to tell Eliot about Michelle and the letters. It was not that she did not trust him – she trusted him absolutely and felt tempted to put it all into his capable hands which would somehow sort it all out – but she feared his displeasure. She imagined the look of disappointment that might cross his face if she made such an allegation against somebody who was, after all, a relation of his.

She couldn't bear to risk losing his good opinion. Everything had changed since the time in the wood when she had poured out her heart to him and he had comforted her as she wept in his arms. Perhaps she had fallen in love with him. She hugged the thought to her like a guilty secret. Nobody must know, most of all Eliot, but at night she would take it out and examine it, this secret. Yet she still loved Alastair, but that was a different matter altogether. Alastair was like herself; she had no illusions about that. He did silly and impetuous things as she did, got hurt and angry and showed it, as she did. He took things to heart and was vulnerable. He was loveable only as an equal.

But Eliot was quite different. He was completely in control. It was hard to define what it was exactly. He had authority. So presumably she liked authority. It was against the spirit of the age and all that, she reflected wryly. On the other hand, it wasn't surprising, she realised, trying to be honest with herself. The only person she had loved from babyhood had been a man who had authority over her: her father.

Life with Eliot would be marvellous, she thought, allowing herself to drift off into fantasy. With Eliot she would be safe and protected. He wouldn't let life buffet her about, she was sure of that. Not that he had ever implied that he wanted to look after her forever, but from the start he had obviously been deadly serious about her.

The next day was Wednesday and he had arranged to come and take her out for a drive if the weather was fine. It turned out to be a lovely sunny afternoon.

"We get this sometimes in Cornwall," he said, as she settled into the passenger seat beside him and they set off slowly down the front drive. "Lovely autumns after awful wet summers."

She smiled up at him.

"You shouldn't do that," he said, glancing down at her. "It could cause an accident."

She sat back in her seat blissfully happy.

"We'll go to Tresenna House," he said. "It has lovely grounds. In the summer you can get tea but the restaurant will be closed now. But we can stroll around the gardens – it's National Trust. That suit you?"

"Whatever you like," she murmured, quite unable to feel anything but total complaisance with whatever he said.

"Good Lord," he exclaimed suddenly. "I quite forgot – *you* were going to do the driving."

"I don't mind; I'm quite happy like this."

She did not want anything to change; just sit and watch his hands on the wheel, feel his shoulder now and then as the bends in the road dictated.

"Nonsense. The object was to keep you up with your driving. There is no time like the present."

He brought the car to a halt at the roadside.

"All right, I'd like to," she said, realising that it was going to be equally pleasant to let him show her how to manage the car, let him teach her things.

"Have you got your specs? I'm not letting you drive without them."

She looked in her bag; blessedly they were there. He got out and she slid over to his seat.

She sat obediently while he explained the gears, making herself pay attention to what he said and not just watch his hands.

They set off slowly, down the road. She made a hideous sound as she changed gears. He put her hand over hers. "Gently," he murmured. "Learn to caress the gear lever."

She did better after that.

She managed to park the car without mishap when they reached the gardens and sat back with a sigh of relief.

"Well done," he said. "You have a feel for it."

"Thank you," she said, ridiculously gratified by his praise.

They seemed to have the gardens to themselves and sat for a while on a south-facing seat looking down over a sloping lawn surrounded by acres of woodland. Behind them was the house, a simple Georgian building soon to be taken over by the Ministry of the Environment for use as an agricultural college.

He took her hand. "I love it here," he said. "It sounds silly but it reminds me of my home and my childhood."

"You were brought up in a place like this?"

"Yes. But it had to be sold for death duties, lack of staff, all the usual reasons. But do you know, whenever I come to a house and grounds like this I feel just a little bit homesick?"

"Oh, I can imagine that. I feel homesick for cities, but it's the same thing really – where you were a child."

"You like towns?"

She nodded.

"I'm glad about that. When I've finished helping out here, I'll probably go back to town life. That's why I just stay on at the pub. Though I suppose it might be worthwhile having a cottage to come back to for holidays, don't you think?"

Her heart beat faster; he was asking her opinion about planning his future.

"What sort of work will you be doing?" she asked as casually as she could, not wanting to seem to be taking too personal an interest. Her voice came out like that of a little girl trying to talk to the grown-ups.

"Something to do with accountancy, I expect. I've a few contacts. In fact, a friend of mine in the import-export business wrote to me only last week; he's looking for a partner."

It all sounded very grand to Professor Cassell's daughter, who knew nothing of the business world.

"Good Lord," Eliot said suddenly. "What am I doing here with you on a perfect afternoon in a beautiful garden talking about business?"

He took her by the hand and led her across the lawn. "Come on, we'll forget all that nonsense," he said. "Let's see if I can still remember the way to the marvellous view of the creek. It's roughly in this direction."

They found it eventually, after walking along various paths through the trees. A nature trail had been marked out and they stopped sometimes to identify trees, about which he obviously knew as little as she did. Suddenly there opened out before them a vista of the blue water of the estuary and behind it the dark green of wooded banks.

"It's breath-taking," she said.

"You are breath-taking," Eliot said quietly.

He was a few yards away from her. He did not move towards her. He just looked at her and held out his arms. "Come here," he said in the same quiet voice.

She seemed to walk towards him in slow motion, as if he were drawing her. It was an incredibly exciting feeling to be drawn to him by this strange power. The power of him, she thought. Then the phrase 'power corrupts' came into her mind and with an excitement even more intense she recognised the seductive power of corruption.

In his arms, she felt as always his extraordinary detachment. There was no flurry about him, nothing in the least resembling the sexual arousal of other men she had known. He was so calm, he was the unmoved cause of all excitement. Sometimes she would open her eyes and see him watching her and instead of destroying the spell it strengthened it. It was as if a third party were watching, yet it only increased her excitement, put her quite at his mercy.

"Keep to the nature trail, Spargo," a man's voice said. "Look out for the Eucalyptus Coccifera which is on the left. It is marked *item ten* on your brochure."

Twenty little boys appeared on the path. They wore the grey shorts and blue blazers of the local prep school and as they passed some raised their caps to Eliot and Ruth who stood aside to let them pass. The master, a tall young man with close-cropped hair and a rucksack, brought up the rear. He looked anxious and gave them an uneasy smile as they exchanged greetings.

"Better be going, anyway," Eliot murmured after the troop had passed. "Back to prison with you."

"The Eucalyptus originates in Australia and Tasmania," the young man was saying. "The Coccifera is a Tasmanian Mountain form. Note the mealy whiteness of the trunk and branches."

His voice faded away.

"Poor sod, what a life," Eliot said.

CHAPTER TEN

"That Sandra Forbes has *such* an enquiring mind," Miss Pool said, coming into the staff room with Ruth. "Do you know, all through my lesson she asked questions? She must have asked at least fifty."

She giggled nervously and, reaching for the tongs, sat down in the armchair and began to mend the fire.

"You don't think," Ruth suggested as diplomatically as she could, "that she was just trying to be a nuisance?"

"On no!" Miss Pool's voice was quite shocked. "She just has an enquiring mind. You could tell she was interested from all the questions she asked, you see. Too interested in a way–"

Her voice trailed off and she peered despondently into the fire, trying to find a chink of light to obliterate.

It was no good, Ruth thought; nothing would shake Puddles's faith in the goodness of human nature, or at least of human nature when young. She was so innocent of all malice herself that she could never understand children. So paradoxically she drew out all that was bad in them.

"Well, I suppose I'd better–" Miss Pool said, as a bell rang. "Are you–?"

"No, I have an unexpected free period; Miss Enders wanted my lot for a double lesson, so naturally I obliged."

After Puddles had gone, she lay back in her armchair and stretched luxuriously. Yesterday there had been Eliot and tomorrow there would be Eliot and today this undeserved bonus of a free period to catch up with piles of marking. It was sunny too and that was rare; she watched the tiny flecks of dust dancing in the bright light that streamed in the window, and felt grateful to fate for bringing her to this school.

The door opened and Michelle came in. She looked surprised when she saw Ruth. "Miss Fairbairn told me to come and get the coffee tray," she explained. "I expect she thought you would all be teaching."

"She reckoned without my free period," Ruth told her. "How is your dress getting on? If it's ready for a fitting I can come down to your room tonight to be your model."

"Oh yes, please, if you are sure you have the time. It has been ready for a little while, but I didn't like to bother you."

They heard footsteps crossing the hall.

"I'm off," Ruth said. "See you tonight."

She was ashamed of herself, that was the truth of it, she told herself as she settled down to mark a pile of books in the study. She had known that Michelle was desperately worried about not hearing from home, and she had done nothing to help her. She should have asked Eliot about it – indeed every time she went out with him she fully intended to – but when it came to the point she could not bring herself to risk upsetting him, particularly just now when he had suggested that she might stay at his pub for half-term. It wasn't exactly a firm invitation; he had just thrown it out as a casual idea. He might not mention it again if she spoiled everything by implying that his relation Miss Fairbairn and his friend Mrs Bland were not above pinching letters that belonged to their staff.

Besides, although when she was in the building Ruth believed in the danger to Michelle, or at least in some kind of mystery, it always seemed absurd once she was away from the place. She couldn't help feeling that maybe they were all just an overwrought bunch of women, too much cooped up together, breeding suspicion and jealousy and dislike. That, no doubt, would be Eliot's opinion and she couldn't help seeing things through his eyes nowadays.

All the same, as she sat at her desk in the study with a pile of books in front of her, and remembered how Michelle's face had lit up when she said she would go to her room tonight, she felt ashamed. She felt even worse about it that evening because Michelle was so determinedly cheerful, although she looked strained. She didn't even mention the letters or refer to Miss Fairbairn. In fact she seemed only interested in talking about Ruth and her plans.

"What will you do at half-term, Ruth?" she asked, as she fitted the dress on to her. "I will stay here."

"I'm not sure," she hedged. "I did think of going to London, but I've had an invitation to stay locally. It might be more of a rest."

Eliot had been at pains to make it clear that she would just be a fellow guest, no more. All the same it did seem a kind of disloyalty to Michelle, siding with one of the school establishment.

"I'm going to rest," Michelle said. "Mrs Bland and Miss Fairbairn are going to the Isles of Scilly for the weekend and all the others will be away from Friday morning, so I am going to do nothing."

"It's what you need. You look terribly tired – and you're thinner."

"We shall see," Michelle said as, with her mouth full of pins, she made a few alterations to the dress. Then she helped Ruth take it off, drawing it gently over her head.

It was typical of Michelle that the only thing she had bought for her room was a long mirror which was propped up under the light. It was second-hand and pockmarked but ideal for dressmaking purposes. She put on the dress and stood in front of it now. Ruth came across and stood behind her.

"You're much thinner round the waist," she said. "I told you that you'd lost weight. You'll have to make the darts bigger, but otherwise it's perfect. It's remarkable really–"

She stopped. Perhaps it was a trick of the light, or just the way Michelle's long hair fell forward like her own after pulling the dress over her head, or perhaps some subconscious connection of ideas was triggered off by seeing her own hands near Michelle's throat as they turned back the collar of the dress. But whatever the reason, she was suddenly sure of something and spoke without stopping to think.

"He meant to kill *you*" she said.

"What do you mean?" Michelle asked, horrified both by the words and the expression on Ruth's face.

"The man – whoever it was. He thought I was you. I was wearing your red coat. We are alike. I stopped under the light but he would only see fair hair, as my head was down looking at my watch, and the red coat. He would assume it was you."

"Especially," Michelle said, "if he was expecting me."

"Oh, no! You don't think she sent you on purpose that night – to be strangled. No, Michelle."

They were talking in whispers. She reached out and took Michelle's hands and they sat for a moment frozen in horror, like two children frightening each other with ghost stories.

"If it is true," Ruth said in as matter-of-fact a voice as she could. "Then two attempts have been made on your life. And both times you've been saved by chance. You've got to get out."

She should have told Eliot, she should have told Eliot.

Michelle shook her head. "No," she said. "I'm not going away. Not until I know why. I want to know about the letters."

"You've heard no more?"

"Nothing."

Partly because she felt guilty that she had done nothing about the letters, partly because she was frightened, Ruth spoke impulsively, "Michelle, we must find those letters. Either Mrs Bland or Miss Fairbairn must have them – unless they've been destroyed. We must get them back."

Even so, she probably wouldn't have said it if she had thought Michelle would agree. She expected her to say it was a mad idea. But the French girl said, "Yes, I have thought of it too. But Miss Fairbairn's room is always locked. I have tried."

"Then we must try Mrs Bland's room first. Though I can't believe *she* can be in on anything like that."

"She was the one who took the letters from you that afternoon."

"Yes, that's true. But that doesn't mean she kept yours. She might easily have given them to Miss Fairbairn to give to you."

They were silent for a moment and then, "If the letters are in Mrs Bland's study, I'll get them," Ruth said, as if it were a simple matter to steal mail from the Headmistress's study.

"You are good to me," Michelle said simply. "No wonder they did not wish us to be friends!"

74

Ruth laughed, feeling strangely relieved now that she was ridding herself of guilt. "We have to think of the best time," she said. "The night before half-term there's a talk for the Sixth Form that Mrs Bland is sure to go to. She'll be stuck up there on the platform with the speaker, so that's her out of the way."

"I can guard Miss Fairbairn," Michelle said. "Unless you do, while *I* go to Mrs Bland's room?"

"No, it's more natural for you to be down here. You see to old Esther and I'll do the burgling. The talk will start at half past seven. After a few minutes I'll go and make sure that Mrs Bland is on the platform, with the staff and plenty of girls between her and the door, then I'll go to her study and search her desk. I'll have to take that," she added, pointing to the torch which she always used when she came down to the basement. "If I find the letters I'll go up and hide them in my room, then come and look for you. You go up and read them, come back and guard Esther while I take them back into the Head's desk before anybody notices."

She laughed and added shakily, "It's quite simple really."

"You have the dangerous part," Michelle said doubtfully. "They are my letters, I think I should take the risk."

"No. It's very important to guard Miss Fairbairn. Where is she usually from eight onwards?"

"Usually up with the Head, but of course that night she won't be. Either she will go to the talk or she will be in her own room."

"Then you just stay within sight of whatever room she is in and if she moves out in the direction of the Head's study, you just get there first and warn me."

"I promise," Michelle said.

They talked over the details and said good-night.

"And if I find nothing," Ruth said cheerfully, "then we must just steal the key of Miss Fairbairn's room and burgle that next."

She picked up the dress from the chair. "We didn't do much with that, did we?" she said, handing it back to Michelle. Then she kissed her friend goodnight and set off quietly down the corridor.

She stopped suddenly; there would be no harm in just going to have a look at the housekeeper's room, just in case they had to search it later. She went slowly, not using the torch but feeling her way with her hands against the wall. The flaking plaster was rough against her fingers; they would soon be covered with white dust. She was by now fairly familiar with the basement passageways and found her way to the housekeeper's room without much difficulty. No light shone from under the door; so Esther Fairbairn was safely installed in the Head's study.

She was about to try the door, when she noticed that almost next to it was another door, slightly ajar. She hesitated and then, thinking that if they did eventually have to burgle the housekeeper's room it would be useful to know the layout of the place, she pushed the door open and shone her torch around the room. It was a small kitchen, presumably for the housekeeper's private use. Quickly her eyes took in the little cooker, sink and table, then she switched off the torch and pulled the door half-closed, as she had found it.

The darkness was more intense after the brief brightness of the torch; she stretched out her hand towards the door of the housekeeper's room, feeling for the door knob. She found it and, very gently, turned it. The door was locked; she stood for a moment, not sure if what she felt was disappointment or relief.

She was just going to set off for her room, when she heard the sound. It was a curious creaking kind of noise, but the terrifying thing about it was that it was so close to her. She pressed herself back against the wall, turning her head to try to make out where the sound came from. It was a noise that she had heard before, she was sure; could it be the shuffling sound that Albert made as he crept along that it reminded her of?

"Well?" Esther Fairbairn's voice said suddenly.

The voice was so near that Ruth almost screamed, but her mouth was dry and incapable of sound.

"Well," the voice said again and it seemed to be almost on top of her, as if in her own head.

"But Esther," she heard Mrs Bland's voice say patiently, "What *can* I say?"

Where were they? Oh, God, had she gone made? Had this terrifying building with its catacombs and atmosphere of coke fumes and hatred driven her mad? She pressed herself against the wall and pushed one fist into her mouth to prevent herself from crying out.

"Come along, have some of this," she heard Mrs Bland say and the creaking sound came again.

Suddenly she understood. They were directly overhead. They were standing in Mrs Bland's study by the service lift, unintentionally talking into the speaking tube. And she, Ruth, was only a foot or two away from the other end of the shaft which must be just inside the little kitchen. Esther Fairbairn had been down here only a few minutes before, made coffee or something, put it into the lift and forgotten to shut the hatch doors. She had heard that creaking sound before; it was on her first day here and it was the sound that the ropes made as they strained to haul up the tea tray. In her relief she wanted to laugh hysterically. She managed to stop herself but could not prevent the trembling of her body.

"Five years," Esther Fairbairn's voice was accusing. "We'll run it for five years, you said, as a school and then–"

"We shall, Esther, I promise you. Just bear with me."

"Four years have gone already," Esther Fairbairn's voice continued ominously, "and with every day that passes you get yourself more involved with this school–"

"But I must, don't you see? The last thing we want to do is let the place run down, draw attention–"

"My God, if you double cross me" the housekeeper burst out furiously. "If you use me to build up this place and then–"

"Esther, my dear Esther," Mrs Bland interrupted and her voice was warm and gentle and had no trace in it of her usual light ironic tone. "Our long-term aims are identical." There was a pause and then with solemn emphasis, she added, "Believe me, Esther, trust me, please."

There was a short silence and then Esther Fairbairn said, with a kind of little girl petulance that amazed Ruth, "Oh, you always get round me. You always get your own way."

"Then let me have my own way now," Mrs Bland said cheerfully, "and let me give you some coffee before it gets cold."

Standing crouched in the corridor below, Ruth heard the sound of liquid being poured. Then the hatch doors were closed and there was silence. She waited for a few minutes, recovering. How stupidly neurotic she'd been! What she had thought was Albert spying on her was a squeaky rope and what she had thought were voices inside her mad head was her employer having some sort of quarrel with her housekeeper. Cursing her overactive imagination, she made her way back to the basement corridor, flashing the torch confidently as she went. One in the main passage she was about to switch on the light when she noticed, in a store room down a side-passage, Albert busy repairing an old desk. The light shone on his bald head and she watched fascinated as he almost flicked the heavy desk up onto his shoulder as if there was no weight in it. Then he shuffled off with his curious slow sideways walk in the direction of some distant back stairs.

She listened for a moment to the pathetic shuffling sound of his laborious progress and reflected what long hours he worked, then she set off once again for her own room. She was just thinking, as she climbed the wide staircase, what extraordinary strength the old man must still have to be able to pick up a desk like that, when a tightness seized her throat. Yet another time that night, revelation struck. Albert could easily lift a girl up off the path so that she seemed to fly through the air; his shoulders and arms were strong enough for that and his hands big enough to finish the job. But if the girl managed to slip away, he would not be able to follow, powerful though he was. He would be the one who could attack but not pursue – in the manner which had seemed to her so inexplicable.

CHAPTER ELEVEN

Everything went according to plan. Ruth watched with satisfaction as the curator of the local museum arrived with various samples of his treasures in a large bag which he carried into the hall. She saw Mrs Bland go in with him, then went up to her room to mark books, in case anybody should suggest that she should go to the talk as well.

Just before eight she picked up the torch and went downstairs. She had taken the precaution of putting on her spectacles, so through the glass doors of the hall she could see them all quite plainly: the senior girls were sitting in rows, a few of the staff among them. At the far end on the platform was the curator and Mrs Bland, nicely hedged in behind a table covered with objects of archaeological interest. The speaker was even now holding up some kind of gold goblet which Mrs Bland was regarding with close attention, her head slightly on one side.

Ruth approached the Head's study from the staff sitting room side; it was less obvious than going through the swing doors from the corridor. She crossed the cold main hall. The door of the Head's study was slightly open. She slipped in.

The fire was burning brightly and illuminated the room. She need not have brought the torch. She shut the door behind her. Nobody would walk into the study uninvited except Miss Fairbairn and the Head: Miss Fairbairn was closely guarded by Michelle and the Head was trapped in the hall by archaeology.

She crossed quickly to the desk and put down the unnecessary torch. It was a knee-hole desk with three drawers on each side. Some instinct made her start with the left-hand side lowest drawer. In it was a pile of letters. The bottom two were in pale blue envelopes. She could hardly believe her luck. She checked the addresses and that the letters were inside. Then she put the rest back exactly as they were.

She hadn't thought where she would hide the letters. She had no pockets. They would slip out if she hid them in her sweater. In the end she tucked them inside her tights. Then she crossed the room and went quickly out, leaving the door slightly open as she had found it.

She could hardly believe it could have been so easy, she thought as she made her way upstairs. Her heart was thumping but she managed to exchange cheerful good-nights with some of the younger girls she met on the stairs on their way to bed. One showed her a book on Robin Hood that she was reading and they looked at some of the illustrations together. It was surprisingly easy to act normally.

At last she was back in her room. She shut the door behind her and leant against it for a moment with relief. Then she removed the letters from her tights, put them in one of the exercise books she was marking and slipped it into the drawer of her table. Then she went to tell Michelle.

The basement was deserted. There was no sign of Michelle or the housekeeper.

She was making her way slowly back to her room when she saw them; through the side door of the dining room she could see the Housekeeper and the French girl in the servery busy with trays and cups and plates. They must be getting refreshments ready for after the talk. Just like old Esther to press-gang Michelle into it. She waited for a few moments, hoping that the housekeeper would go away, but it was no good. They seemed to be making sandwiches together now. The best thing would be to read the letters herself and make notes and get them back into the Head's study before the end of the talk. It was better than trusting her luck too far. Really she'd been very lucky up till now, she thought, as she sat down at the table and pulled out the book with the letters. The fire being bright enough to see by had been an unexpected bonus. She hadn't even needed the torch!

The torch! Where was it? A vision of the torch, large and red and with her name clearly marked on the handle, came into her mind as it sat there in the middle of the Head's desk.

In less than a minute she was back on the ground floor: check, the Head was still in the hall; she couldn't see very clearly as she had left her spectacles in her room, but she could make out that there were still two shapes behind the table on the platform and the audience was still sitting in rows. In the servery, two people who could only be Michelle and Miss Fairbairn were still carving up sandwiches. She was outside the Head's study now, the door was slightly ajar, as she had left it. It only took a second to cross the room and grab the torch.

The telephone, as if triggered by some connecting mechanism, rang out as the touched the torch. She jumped back and then reached out to take it off the hook; anything to stop the noise.

Then she thought better of it and almost ran out of the room, the accusing bell ringing out behind her like a burglar alarm.

Outside the door, she hesitated, afraid of meeting somebody if she went back to the main school corridor. The telephone bell was the one thing which might bring one of the staff hurrying to the study, some helpful old trouble-maker anxious to please. So instead she turned and climbed up the stairs of Private House, intending to return to the main school via the swing doors on the dormitory corridor. The telephone stopped ringing as she reached the first landing. It had been a false alarm; never mind, better safe than sorry. She looked up: at the top of the second flight of stairs a figure was standing.

Ruth stood, as if paralysed, staring back at it. It was a small greyish figure; a child in a dressing gown maybe. It had no right to be in Private House – but neither had she. She licked her lips and managed to say, "You should be in bed." The figure did not move. She began to climb the stairs as confidently as she could and asked, "Is anything wrong?" Then, drawing nearer, she saw that it was only a vacuum cleaner which one of the cleaning staff must have left at the top of the stairs.

Cursing her short sight, she crossed the Head's landing and slipped through the swing doors. There was nobody about as she ran up the last flight of stairs. Oh, the blessed peace of one's own room, she thought, as she collapsed into the chair, the torch on the floor beside her.

At first she felt illogically guilty about opening Michelle's letters, then merely puzzled. They were very hard to make out, the writing was of the kind that consists of parallel strokes with occasional loops. There was much reference to people who were presumably relations. There was something about a will and the ownership of land. The second letter started with M. Guyomarc'h expressing surprise that she had not written – so they were intercepting Michelle's letters both ways. There was more about the will. There was an address, for a Monsieur and Madame Fournier, to which Michelle was to go in London.

Ruth copied the address into her diary, intending to return the letters at once to the Head's desk. But then it seemed absurd, after all this trouble, for Michelle not to read them. It would be a bitter disappointment for her to know that Ruth had actually held them in her hands and then taken them back without letting her see them herself. The more she thought about the wrongs being heaped upon Michelle the more defiant she felt. I'll get the letters back somehow or other later tonight, she thought confidently, everything has been so easy up till now.

The importance of the letters was now evidently so great that she didn't dare to leave them in her room. She hid them again in her tights; they crackled against her stomach as she ran downstairs. If she could just get Michelle out of there for a moment, she thought, she could hand her the letters in the loo.

The curator had finished his talk. The neat rows of chairs had been pushed back and the girls were standing in groups. Michelle and Miss Fairbairn were handing around sandwiches and cups of coffee.

"It was an excellent talk, was it not?" Miss Enders remarked to Ruth as she slipped into the hall. She murmured something noncommittal and walked across to Michelle at the other side of the room.

"I'm starving," she said loudly and then whispered, "I've got the letters."

"These are egg sandwiches," Michelle said, and added in a whisper, "Where are they?"

"Here," Ruth murmured, patting her stomach.

"You've *eaten* my letters?"

Ruth snorted with laughter. "That's only in spy stories," she said. "Come up to my room later, if I can't–"

Before she could explain, Miss Fairbairn bore down on them looking disapproving, as always, and told Michelle to go and get another jug of coffee. The French girl went meekly off to do as she was told.

Ruth moved quickly away and joined a group of VI formers; she felt safer with the children than with the staff. Guiltily she heard the crackling of letters as she walked. Why should she feel like a thief? Dammit it was the Head and the Housekeeper who were the thieves. In a moment of sadness she realised she hated to think of Mrs Bland like that. She was quite happy to believe any evil of Esther Fairbairn, but Mrs Bland – no.

She wished Eliot were here; she could trust him with the letters to return. The thought of him reassured her. There was another life outside this school, thank goodness. This weekend, she would tell him all about it, for she had told him she would stay with him at the pub. It would all be solved by then; she thought with satisfaction of how it would be to tell Eliot of her exploits and to receive his praise. After all, Miss Fairbairn was only his very distant relation and Mrs Bland none at all. It was her, Ruth, that he really cared about.

At last it was all over; Miss Fairbairn had led Michelle off to the servery, Mrs Bland had led away the curator, the girls had gone to the dormitories and the staff to their rooms. Ruth went upstairs to await Michelle.

It was after ten o'clock when the French girl came. She looked exhausted; Ruth pushed a chair towards her.

"I can't understand it," Michelle said. "Miss Fairbairn is being so kind. She is finishing the dishes by herself and tells me that tomorrow I must stay in bed and rest."

"You need it," Ruth said and handed her the letters.

Michelle read the letters intently, never glancing up. Ruth tried not to watch her, pretending to mark books, but all the time her eyes were drawn to the French girl, who sat there so composedly. It was impossible to believe that anyone should have tried to kill her. There must be some explanation of it all. She saw Michelle fold up the letters, carefully replace them in the envelopes and put them back in the exercise book, doing everything neatly and methodically as she always did.

"Well?"

"In the first letter," Michelle explained, "he tells me about this land. It seems that my grandmother, who had, as I told you, Mrs Bland by her first husband and my mother by her second, preferred the daughter of her first marriage. So she left her money to Mrs Bland, and to my mother she left the house and garden, which had been left to her by a relation and let out as a school. She thought it of little value, and perhaps she wanted to tempt my mother back to England at some later time. I do not know. *This* house and *this* garden," she explained with a wide gesture that took in Ruth's garret.

Ruth, who had assumed that the land was somewhere in France, stared at her in amazement.

"You mean that this school really belongs to your mother?"

"It did."

"But then now–"

"Now it becomes mine. At least when I am twenty-one next Monday-"

"Michelle! You never told me it was your birthday!"

"Well, I was afraid you might feel obliged to stay – and really there is nothing to celebrate."

"Well, many happy returns of next Monday. Go on about the land and everything –"

"You see my mother never did anything about it, never saw it even. She never came to England. Once she married, she was a Frenchwoman. All things English she forgot. She did not mind if her stepsister wished to use the house as a school, why should she? It was no use to her and nobody thought that it was of much value then. In fact they thought it was a burden to keep in repair such an old building."

"But now it's worth a fortune as development land. I heard somebody say it would sell for a quarter of a million pounds."

For the first time Michelle looked frightened. Ruth understood why: it was the sort of money people might commit murder for.

"Michelle," she said. "Stay up here tonight."

"No, it will make them suspicious."

"You've got to get out, Michelle, really you have. Look, tomorrow everybody will go away. Why don't you just walk out on Saturday?"

"Walk out?"

"Yes, just go down to Truro as if you're shopping and then catch the train to London and go to that address."

Michelle nodded. "I don't know if I have enough money."

"Look, here's ten pounds. It's all right, you can pay me back. You see, if Miss Fairbairn thinks you are here for the rest of the term she's no reason to try anything on until they're back from the Scilly Isles, so you're perfectly safe. So long as I get these letters back they've no cause for suspicion."

"I'd almost forgotten the letters. Oh, Ruth, what trouble I have put you in. I don't like to go away just like that."

"You must, Michelle. You must see it now. Before those attacks on you could have been accidents, but now there is a motive."

She copied the address on to a piece of paper and gave it to Michelle, with the money.

"There," she said. "That's all settled."

"I should write to my friend in France and tell him all this?"

"I shouldn't," Ruth said, "wait until you're in London. If they found the letter or anything it's not worth taking risks."

Michelle nodded. "And when shall we get the letters back to the Head's study?" she asked.

"Leave that to me," Ruth said with more confidence than she felt.

She carried the letters in the exercise book just in case she met anybody on her way to the study, but she need not have worried. The whole school was sleeping. The landing lights were always left on and they made a glow sufficient for her to see her way down the long corridor. She gave the swing doors a gentle push. They did not give. She pushed harder; they were as firm as a rock. They were locked. It had never occurred to her that the whole of Private House was locked at night. She hadn't even realised it was possible to lock swing doors. She went up the first flight of stairs and tried the door on the next landing. Locked. Miserably she returned to her own room.

Could she risk not returning them? Could she gamble on the Head not looking in her desk before going away tomorrow? She dared not. If the loss of the letters were discovered, Michelle would be in immediate danger. Michelle's one advantage was that nobody thought she knew anything. She must not lose that advantage.

Ruth put the exercise book under her pillow, went to bed and slept badly.

Breakfast was a noisy affair the next morning. No sooner was it over than cars began to arrive to take the children away for half-term. Two coachloads of girls went off to the station, some went by taxi. Farewells were shouted, parents embraced children. Brothers arrived, looking embarrassed. Small Anna Speight – who had shown her the Robin Hood book last night – waited alone and anxious in the hall for her father to come. He was a widower – a nice man, Ruth remembered, whom she had met soon after she came to Polglaze. At last his car appeared at the top of the drive. Ruth watched through the staff sitting room window as the little girl shot like a bullet out of the front door. A door slammed. The widowed father stood by the car, arms outstretched and the child hurtled herself into them. Ruth got up involuntarily as if to stop her; inside her head a voice was warning the child, "Don't trust him so. Don't let him be your whole world. He'll let you down."

She stood aghast at her own reaction. And with so much else to think about too, she told herself, clutching the exercise book with its guilty contents to her. Surely she had more pressing problems to think about than the emotional security of Anna Speight?

The two Miss Enders had brought their car round from the back and parked it in the front drive. They were setting off, taking Miss Pool with them. Mrs Hamilton-Smythe had already gone. The Head and Miss Fairbairn appeared from the front door, evidently coming out to see the senior staff off the premises. They were all standing round the car.

"Now!" Ruth thought and, not allowing herself time to think, made boldly for the Head's study. The room seemed unnaturally still. The grate was empty and clean, the room cold. She crossed over to the desk; everything looked exactly as it had done the night before. She slid the letters out of the exercise book and into the drawer, carefully replacing them under the pile of envelopes.

She was starting back across the room when she heard voices in the hall. She had miscalculated. The Head and Esther Fairbairn must have kept their farewells brief and were already returning. She thought of climbing out of the window; there was no time. They were coming into the room. She slipped behind the curtains instead. They were long and made of thick velvety stuff.

"Well, everybody's off," Mrs Bland said thankfully.

"Except us and our two young friends," Ruth heard Esther Fairbairn reply. "I have advised Michelle to stay in bed today, she is tired and has a cold."

"How kind you are to her – it takes a load off my mind!"

"Don't worry about Michelle – I'll take care of her."

It wasn't clear to Ruth, behind her curtain, whether the Housekeeper's words contained a promise or a threat. She would have given much to have seen the expression on her face as she spoke.

"I've told Albert he can have the weekend off," went on Miss Fairbairn, "but he won't go the obstinate old man."

"He's very conscientious about that boiler. And I suppose the poor old chap has nowhere to go."

"There's no need to feel sorry for him. He has a nephew near Truro he can visit if he wants to. As for the boiler, if he turned the heating down the automatic feed would take care of that."

There was a pause and then Mrs Bland said suddenly, "Coffee would be nice. Let's have it early, shall we?"

"I'll get it now."

Let them both go, please God, Ruth prayed behind the curtain. She heard the door being opened and quietly closed.

Mrs Bland cleared her throat.

"Miss Cassell," she said calmly. "It would be so much easier for us both, would it not, if you came out of hiding?"

She couldn't believe it. She wanted to deny that she was there. Then, telling herself that she must be as calm as possible and summon up all her acting ability, she emerged.

"I'm so sorry," she said contritely.

"I'm sure," Mrs Bland said coldly, "that there is a perfectly satisfactory explanation. I would rather have it than an apology."

"I wanted to speak to you," she said earnestly, "about something very important. I came in, thinking you were here –".

Mrs Bland watched her, eyes slightly narrowed, mouth unsmiling, and said nothing.

"When you came in with Miss Fairbairn I didn't want to have to speak about it

84

in front of anyone else. I mean it's so important that I wanted to speak to you alone – so I hid."

At least a shadow of doubt broke the flat hostility of Mrs Bland's expression.

"And what was that very important topic that you wished to ask me about?"

It would have to be something pretty big; no good saying something about house marks or lost property.

"I want to leave," she said.

Mrs Bland stared at her in consternation. It had worked!

"But I thought you were happy with us? You seemed quite settled."

"I wouldn't go immediately of course," Ruth said, taken aback by the success of her ploy. "I mean I'd stay until you got somebody else."

"Thank you," Mrs Bland said grimly. "I am aware of the terms of your contract and have no intention of waiving them."

It confused her, this sudden return of hostility. "It's a personal matter," she said. "Nothing to do with work. I like teaching, and the children and everything."

Mrs Bland's expression softened. "Then let us hope that your personal affairs will so arrange themselves that you will stay with us after all," she said. "Shall we talk about it again after half-term? I think we are perhaps all rather tired and it is not the best of times to make important decisions. Come and see me next Tuesday. Shall we say after lunch?"

Ruth almost sighed aloud with relief. By next Tuesday Michelle would be safely away and all danger over. The letters were back in the desk, all was well with the world. Even walking into Esther Fairbairn and nearly sending the coffee tray flying out of her hands did not dismay her, as she walked confidently back across the hall.

CHAPTER TWELVE

Michelle was sitting sewing by her gas fire, in her dressing gown, when Ruth went into her room to say good-bye.

"I thought you were having the day in bed," Ruth remarked.

"I am. I am just finishing the dress then I'll have a snack and go back to bed."

After she had told her about returning the letters, Ruth said, "Have you everything you need for tomorrow?"

Michelle nodded. "I shall walk out as I am," she said. "I shall wear this dress and the red coat."

"Never mind what you'll wear–"

"I always mind what I wear," Michelle interrupted her.

"You're incorrigible; you'd fuss on about your own shroud if it didn't fit properly."

"Of course," Michelle told her calmly. "It matters that things should be done properly."

"At the moment all that matters is your safety. Don't forget that."

"All right," Michelle reassured her casually, "but really I am very safe here."

"Shall I call in before I leave this evening?"

"No, don't worry about me so. I'll probably be asleep anyway."

"Then I won't disturb you again. I'll be off now – I've got stacks of work to do. Don't write to me here, Michelle. I'll ring that number in London. Good luck."

"Good-bye. I can't thank you enough – you know it?"

"Silly," Ruth said awkwardly. She kissed Michelle good-bye and went out quickly.

Back in her room she tried to close her mind to it all, to thoughts of Michelle as much as to thoughts of Eliot. Four sets of books to be marked, she noticed with horror. It was all very well, but work had to be coped with; you couldn't say, "Sorry children that your work is unmarked because I have been preoccupied with my lover and with thwarting murderesses."

Murderesses! No, it couldn't be. In the context of school and lessons it seemed hysterical even to think such words. Maybe it was all a succession of accidents, of coincidences. But the letters? Was it perhaps possible that those two women were simply trying to postpone the day when Michelle had to know she owned all this land? It didn't necessarily mean that they would harm her. Perhaps they just feared trouble with French lawyers and were going to try to reach some kind of agreement. Perhaps the tower steps just needed repairing and perhaps her attacker in the wood was only a stray maniac.

Whatever the truth of it, she told herself, work had to go on and next week she would have to teach the Upper VI about Henry VIII; the only essay which she'd done at the university on that period was one on the fiscal policy of Tudor chancellors and would be no help at all.

Eliot came early. He stood in the doorway, arms outstretched, and said, "Come here" and she moved into them like a sleepwalker. Oh Eliot, Eliot obliterater of thoughts about the Tudor monarchs, the Wars of the Roses and even the French Revolution. Oh Eliot, who even makes me forget murder and stolen letters and the danger to my friend.

She packed quickly while he sat and watched her. He carried her case downstairs and out into the car.

"You're going to drive," he said. "Got your specs?"

"Yes," she said, getting into the driver's seat obediently, like a child.

"Good girl."

They drove out to Perranporth and walked on the sands. It was cold and windy. Fine sand blew against her cheeks, making them sting. She turned and walked with her back to the wind, her hair blowing forward over her face. Eliot stretched out his arms and she leaned back against the wind, holding his hand and thinking, this is heaven; I shall remember this for ever.

"It's getting cold," Eliot said. "And your shoes are ridiculous. We'll go back to the pub now. I'll drive. You're going to be spoilt from now on."

She laughed and leant against him, tucking herself under his arm, sheltering against him like a rock.

The pub was at the top of a long lane and Eliot was evidently the only resident. She realized that he had given up his room to her. It was a modern extension, a large bedroom with a bathroom of its own and a telephone by the bed.

"It's real Hollywood stuff," she exclaimed, impressed.

"Well, Bill, the owner, is looking to the future. He says one day people will want a bathroom all to themselves in a hotel, no more trailing down the corridor with a towel over your arm, looking for a bathroom. He's mad, of course, it'll never catch on. This is Cornwall not New York, but still it suits me if he deludes himself like that. I'm very comfortable here. And he's installed a television set in the lounge. Mind you, it doesn't work very well, reception's pretty bad."

"But really, Eliot, you shouldn't have given up your room for me."

"You are to have the best of everything," he told her. "And I'm not exactly roughing it. My bedroom's just down there and the bathroom's opposite. But I wanted you to have this view."

"Lovely," she said, giving it a cursory glance. Without her spectacles she had but the vaguest impression of blue and green.

"I'll tell you something," he said gently. "I like spoiling you. Do you know you *need* spoiling? You just call out to be looked after."

"Do I?"

"Yes, and we'll start by giving you a drink. Do you mind if I use that telephone later, by the way? There is a public one but it's well – rather public."

"Of course I don't mind. Goodness, it's your room really!"

They went down to the bar where Eliot introduced her to Bill. He seemed to know Eliot well. But of course he would; this was where Eliot lived, where he came back to at night and slept. Being here with him here was almost like being in his home.

Eliot and Bill talked about the dinner menu, the weather forecast and cricket. She didn't join in much, just watched Eliot's face and enjoyed hearing his voice.

"You go along to the lounge and I'll bring you a drink in there," he told her. "You can sit by the fire and watch the television while I go and sort out a few things in my room. Then I'll join you."

"All right," she said. "Anything you like."

As she went out she heard Bill murmur, "Nice bird that. You're the lucky one."

She flushed. Was that how it seemed to Bill? Was that how it would seem to anybody?

Was that how it really was? She walked out quickly, down the corridor and into the lounge. Eliot followed her, put her drink down on the table beside her, turned on the television set, touched her lightly on the cheek and left her.

The television flickered and she could make no sense of the programme. She got up and began to walk round the room. Phrases like a nice bird and an easy lay wouldn't leave her alone.

She walked restlessly over to the window. Oh hell, what did it matter what life seemed like through the eyes of a man like Bill? She turned off the television. She wanted to go to the loo anyway, she thought and went out. She tried the one at the end of the corridor. It was locked. She went upstairs. The one at the top of the stairs was engaged too. Then she remembered that there was one in her own private bathroom, so she went there instead.

She looked around the bathroom as she sat. It was obviously newly done, all got up in pink and very pretty. Everything that could be boarded in or covered up, had been. The partition walls must be paper thin, though. They had tried to fix a holder to the wall for the toilet roll but it had pulled away leaving a hole edged with torn wallpaper. The basin was one of those small round metal ones surrounded with pretence wood. Vanitory basin, that's what they called it. Must be a cross between vanity and sanitary. Funny words these plumbing people invent. Like low level suite. Sounds like a collapsed blancmange.

Somebody opened the bedroom door. Must be the maid coming to turn down the bed. She listened, embarrassed. Then she heard the telephone being dialled, then Eliot's voice. It was awful; she didn't want to eavesdrop, she thought, getting up all flustered. It would be the second time today, she realised, remembering Mrs

Bland's curtains – and it was a very different thing to listen to Eliot. If he found out he'd despise her – but this time it really wasn't her fault.

"Everything under control," his voice said. "No troubles, no hitches."

Probably some business deal, she thought, to do with his accountancy. It was dreadful to eavesdrop all the same. She must let him know she was there. Pull the plug. She put her hand on the lever of the low level suite.

"Of course I will," Eliot's voice said. "My dear girl, have some confidence in me, will you?"

A woman! He was talking to a woman! She took her hand off the handle of the low level suite.

"I know. I muffed it once. Don't rub it in."

He was speaking in a knowing kind of voice to this woman; the sort of voice men like Bill use.

" Well, it's in your capable hands this time. How are the dear old Sillies?"

Perhaps he was talking to some chance acquaintance, who had elderly parents. Perhaps it was the elderly parents that he knew and was enquiring after. Then it was all right. It would be just like Eliot to ring up to enquire about the welfare of some old people he was concerned for, she thought, putting her hand on the handle again.

"Well, I told you you shouldn't have gone by helicopter."

Scillies! Ye Gods, he was talking to Mrs Bland – or Esther Fairbairn. He was in the conspiracy. Eliot was. So this was the way he talked to them when they were alone. It *couldn't* be Esther Fairbairn, after what he had said about her. The voice didn't fit, it was quite the wrong tone. It must be Mrs Bland.

"I'll tell you something. It's costing me a pretty penny, this weekend lark. You're going to have to raise my expense allowance, old girl. What's that?" he laughed. "Well, you know me, not above mixing business and pleasure."

There was silence; presumably whoever she was at the other end had a lot to say.

"Right you are then," Eliot replied, "you'd better go before she notices. Same sort of situation this end. But glad to know you left everything in order at school. You'll have to be back on Monday morning? I shan't see you before Tuesday: unless the storm breaks before and I'm called in. You're in for quite a time you know, so make the most of the break. Good-bye."

She heard the click of the receiver being replaced, she heard the bedroom door close. She could hardly move for horror. What a fool she'd been. Must get out of here. If he goes downstair's and finds me missing, he'll get suspicious, come back here. She imagined how he would look as the realisation dawned upon him. She recalled how hard his eyes could be. She was suddenly terrified of him and his anger. She remembered how he had said that the Fairbairns were a murderous lot when roused. He was related to the Fairbairns.

Nobody in the corridor, nobody on the stairs. In no time she was back in the lounge, had turned on the television and was sitting in the chair. The same mindless show was going on. To her amazement she saw that she had only been gone ten minutes. She saw him come in, kept herself low in the chair.

"Look," he said. "I've brought another drink for you."

He put the full glass down on the table at her side.

"Lovely," she said, "I've hardly finished the first."

She drained the glass.

"Don't move. You finish watching that. I'll look at the paper."

She breathed again. So she had time to think. Who had it been on the phone? Whichever it was, the other one was not in on it. Could it really be Mrs Bland who was in league with Eliot? It must be. And the aim was to keep her, Ruth, out of the way. That was the only reason Eliot had asked her for the weekend. But why? Presumably so that Michelle would be alone when they returned on Monday. Thank God that Michelle would be safely away on Saturday morning. They would find their bird flown.

And she would go too. It had all been a plot, a pretence, all his kindness, his fatherly concern. Fatherly, fatherly. Shame overwhelmed her as she thought how stupid she'd been. She'd turned her back on those who really cared for her, on Alastair, on her father and on the kindly woman whom he had come to love. She should have rejoiced for him, knowing that a daughter cannot be a wife, but she'd thought only of her own selfish hurt. If only she'd stayed with them, never bolted to Polglaze. If only she could be there, safely at home with them both, now. Tears of regret and humiliation filled her eyes. She reached surreptitiously into her bag and took out a handkerchief.

No, this wouldn't do, she told herself; she must forget all that, she must plan. Besides if she hadn't come to Polglaze there wouldn't have been anybody to help Michelle. Think positive, Ruth.

Money. She'd given most of it to Michelle. She squinted into her wallet, keeping it hidden in her bag. About three pounds and – her ticket to London. There was a sleeper reservation too, but she wouldn't need that; she'd escape and catch an evening train. Saved. Oh, the relief of seeing that ticket. The forgotten ticket which Alastair had bought for her when he came. Oh, Alastair, you bought it and gave it to me and we were happy then. God, what a fool she'd been. Thank goodness that at least she hadn't cashed it in at the station. Not that that was due to any wisdom – only forgetfulness.

But how was she going to get to the station. Escape? Eliot's car. It was round at the back. It could be driven off without attracting attention. It was dark already. Or could she pretend to want to go back to school for something. Hopeless, he'd insist on taking her. She would just have to distract him and escape. She sat making her plans and the film flickered in front of her shortsighted eyes.

CHAPTER THIRTEEN

"Seven o'clock," she said, stretching and yawning.

He got up immediately and came to stand over her.

"So?"

"So it is time to get ready for dinner."

"You look ready enough now."

"How am I supposed to take that?"

"Any way you like," he said, leaning over her to run his fingers gently down the curve of her cheek, along her neck.

"I'll tell you exactly what we're going to do," she said with mock firmness.

"All right, bossy boots. I'll do anything you say."

"We're going upstairs to have baths; me in my private one, you in yours that you have to share with the rest of the world."

"All right, if you insist."

"I need a long, slow soak to wash away all my schoolmarminess."

"That sounds promising."

"Then we'll have a drink and be just in time for the meal Bill's planned for half past eight."

They climbed the narrow winding stairs hand in hand, close together. Then she disengaged herself, kissed him briefly on the cheek and went to her bedroom. Quickly she checked that she had everything she needed in her bag, then she ran her bath, put on a bath cap, took off her sweater and bra, wrapped a towel round her shoulders and waited until she heard Eliot come out of his bedroom. Then she opened her door and called to him. He was wearing his dressing gown. She could hear his bathwater running.

"Want a book?" she called out. He came and took the paperback out of her hand.

"My favourite thriller writer too," he said. "You think of everything."

She smiled up at him.

"It suits you, that towel," he murmured and moving towards her gently laid his hand on one partly exposed breast.

"Have a good bath," she said, pushing him away. She bolted the door in case he should try to force an entrance; it would spoil everything if he caught a glimpse of the trousers and outdoor shoes that graced her lower half in readiness for a quick getaway.

She waited until she heard him lock himself in his bathroom and then dressed quickly and ran along to his bedroom. His trousers were on a chair by his bed. Two bunches of keys were in his pocket: she took the smaller one, on which she recognised the key of the car.

She went back to her room, left only a bedside lamp on, so that the light showed under the bathroom door. If he should call in he would think she was still in the bath. The longer the delay, the better. Then, making sure that all the corridor lights were off, she crept down the backstairs and out into the yard.

Eliot's car started easily. She was used to its ways, of course, she thought, reflecting on the irony that Eliot himself had taught her to drive it. She kept the lights off until she as well down the drive and then turned them on and accelerated. It had all gone very easily; she had half an hour's start at least. She tried not to think of his anger when he realised she had gone. She tried not to think of the hard eyes, softened hitherto when directed towards her. But she knew how he could look. She would not think of it.

She wished she knew if there was an evening train to London. She had a feeling that there was one at nine or ten. There was always the sleeper, of course, but she wanted to get away as soon as possible. She would call in at the station and find out, then drive the car into town and leave it there; she wanted to leave no clue for Eliot to find. She pictured herself walking the deserted streets from the town up to the station and Eliot drawing up at the kerb side – in Bill's car perhaps. She shivered. She would leave the car and get a taxi.

She wished she could let Michelle know. She might even take her with her. No, that would be stupid. No point in their both arriving in London in the small hours. But she wished she had let her know, all the same. She would! She would soon be passing the drive up to school, it was on her way, only a few minutes' detour. She stopped the car, tore a page out of her diary, wrote on it what she was planning to do and set off for school.

She felt safe in the car; the patch of road ahead that was graced by her own headlights seemed to belong to her. She realised at last why all the oncoming cars dazzled her. They were flashing her because she didn't dip her lights. She had never driven the car after dark before so it hadn't occurred to Eliot to teach her how to dip the lights. She thought of how she had deceived him and felt a flush of guilt. Then she though of the extent of his greater deceit; she would have liked to feel hatred of him, but only felt fear and something that must be self-disgust.

She drove round the back of the school, knowing that the front door would be locked. She parked the car and made her way down the area steps, dimly lit by the moon. The door was stiff and for a moment she thought that it was locked. Then, to her relief, it opened with a loud creaking. She wasn't sure if Albert was here or not, so felt her way along the corridor without turning on the lights. When she reached Michelle's room there was no light shining from within. She stopped down to push the note under the door. It wouldn't go. She knelt down. There was some rough material like carpet lying in a roll at the bottom of the door. Michelle must have put it there to keep out the draught or something. Fool that she was: of course Michelle couldn't do it from the outside! In a panic she turned the handle and threw herself against the door, and fell violently into the room.

Michelle was lying on the bed apparently sound asleep. The room was full of gas. She ran to turn it off, but realised that she couldn't get near enough so overpowering was the smell. Instead she dashed across to the bed, grabbed Michelle round the middle and dragged her across the room.

The French girl's arms and legs trailed along the ground as if she were a dummy. Her poor hands knocked against the furniture. She must get her out into the fresh air, she must get her to hospital. In the corridor she managed to get a better grip on her by getting her arms under Michelle's and dragging her backwards, her legs trailing. Oh God, she is like a broken doll. They have murdered her. Murder, murder a voice was screaming insider her head.

She got her out of the door and on to the area steps. The cold night air struck her like a blessing. Then she heard a car.

It was Eliot, she knew it. She knew it by the way he drove with a flourish up the front drive, stopping with a furious screech of brakes and scattering of gravel. A car door slammed. Oh God, he would find the door locked and would come round to the back. He will kill us both. Here at the back of these gloomy buildings among the dustbins and black drain pipes, near the railings of these basement steps, he will kill us.

But he didn't come. Of course, he must have a key to the front door. There had been another key ring in his pocket: she had seen it. She listened, straining her ears. Would he go up to her room or come down to the basement? He must have gone up. It was herself he was after; she pictured him in a blind fury, tearing up to her room. It wouldn't take him long to see that she was not there.

Frantically she pulled Michelle up the steps, banging her against the iron rungs. Oh God, her poor legs, she'll be bruised all over. Do dead people bruise? She didn't know. She knew nothing useful. Her education, it seemed now to Professor Cassell's daughter, had been long and pricey and useless. It had taught her none of the important things such as what to do with people full of gas or how to know if somebody is dead or not.

Somehow she got Michelle into the car, pushing her, pulling her, flinging in odd bits of her that kept flopping out again. She shut the doors as quietly as she could and gently started the car, lights off. Once out of the grounds and on to the road, she felt safer. There were other cars about, help was at hand. Please God, let Michelle not be dead.

There was a car behind her as she drove into the town. Could it be Eliot in Bill's car? He would recognise his own car so easily, know its number. She must get to the hospital as quickly as possible. In the hospital they would both be safe. The driver behind overtook her: it was not Eliot.

The smell in the car was dreadful. Poor Michelle, gas seemed to be seeping out of every pore of her body. She wondered if she should have stopped to get a blanket. No, that might hold the gas in. The more air the better, she thought, winding down the window.

Suddenly she thought of Albert. She had not turned off the gas tap and she had left Michelle's door wide open. The gas would spread along the basement corridors; it would find its way to the room where the old man lay on his sacks. But she couldn't go back to that building, she couldn't. Anyway, meek and pathetic though he seemed, had he not attempted murder that night in the grounds? Under orders, maybe, but murder all the same. Let him take his chance with the gas.

It was raining as she turned up Infirmary Hill. She drove into the hospital grounds and parked outside the door marked casualty. She climbed out, weak with relief that the first stage of saving Michelle was safely accomplished. A man in uniform appeared immediately.

"Oh, please," she began, running towards him.

"You can't park here, Miss," he said severely. "Here is reserved for ambulances."

"But –"

"Perhaps you did not observe the notice?"

"She's ill," was all she could manage to say and pushed past him. Soon it was out of her hands. Porters got Michelle out of the car, carrying her on a stretcher. An appalling whiff of gas accompanied her on every stage of her journey. Ruth watched the smelly burden that had once been her friend being wheeled away under a sheet and was filled with despair. They have killed her, she thought, they have killed her and it is all my fault. I let it happen. Two warnings were not enough. I found reasons, I ignored instinct. I wanted Eliot to love me, so I did not like to accuse his friends. Therefore I let this happen.

She was sitting on a bench, waiting miserably. A nurse came up. "Are you a relation?" she asked.

"No, I'm just a friend."

A poor sort of friend. The only friend Michelle had in the whole of England. Professor Cassell's daughter had made a pretty poor job of caring for the stranger in our midst.

"She'll be all right," the nurse said. "Two days intubation and she'll be back to normal. She'll have a bad head though for days. Silly girl – a love affair I suppose?"

Ruth stared, then understood. "It wasn't suicide," she began. She was about to say it was murder. They wouldn't believe her, they would think her mad.

"Who are her next of kin?" the nurse asked.

Mrs Bland was her next of kin.

"I don't know," Ruth said.

Michelle was still in danger. They might put her in a little room by herself. She imagined Michelle's aunt arriving to visit. She would come with her two friends and they would have Michelle at their mercy in the little room. They would come armed with deadly flowers and poisoned fruits.

"Please," she asked, "will she be in a big ward?"

"Of course," the nurse said. Then she hesitated, "Do you mean you wish her to go privately? It could be arranged. Mr Brearly could be in charge of her."

"No, no I want her to be in a ward with other people. She would be," her voice sank, "– safer."

"Quite," the nurse said. "All of us nurses think that our patients are safer in the ward."

"Then I'll go now," Ruth said, "and leave her in your hands."

She arranged that she would ring the hospital the next morning to see what progress Michelle had made and, if she could be discharged, come and collect her on Monday morning. She did not say that she was catching the sleeper, for fear of Eliot following the trail. She gave her address as Polglaze School.

"Polglaze School?" the nurse remarked. "We see a lot of your Mrs Rhodes here."

"Helen Rhodes?"

"Yes," the nurse said, obviously glad of somebody to chat to on a rather dull night shift.

"She brings her husband in for treatment after school. He's a cripple, you know."

"No, no, I didn't know," Ruth said. I am learning a lot tonight, she thought. So that is why she dashes off; and I thought it was frivolity.

At the door of the hospital she hesitated, fearful of leaving her sanctuary. But she must; the sleeper left in half an hour. She peered out into the rain. No sign of anybody lurking about. It was tempting to leave the car here and walk to the station. But Eliot would be hunting the town for his car and if he found it in the hospital car park it would lead him straight to Michelle. She could imagine him enquiring of the nurse if there had been any admissions, using his charming smile, rather anxious and concerned. The nurses would be all too willing to help him. He would soon guess who the girl was who was admitted with the gas poisoning. Perhaps she should have warned the nurse. But she had no proof. They would think that she was just trying to cover up her friend's attempted suicide. They would discountenance murder, as the police had discountenanced rape.

She drove the car into the centre of the town and parked it. If it stayed there tomorrow morning, Eliot would get a parking ticket, she thought with satisfaction as she crossed to the taxi rank.

She leant back in her corner of the taxi, imagining Eliot's face peering in at her from every passing car. She remembered the sound of him crashing up to her garret room. He was in a state of blind fury, she knew it. He might do anything.

She leant forward and asked the taxi driver to get as near as possible to the station entrance, muttering something about her bad leg. There were ten minutes to go before the train came in. She would soon be safe, alone in her first class sleeper; God bless Alastair for that indulgent thought. Where could she otherwise have hidden herself away for the night? She longed for the moment when she would close the door behind her; after that nobody could get at her, as she sped on her way to London.

She was expecting the station to be unmanned, as it had been when Alastair caught the sleeper, but the booking clerk was waiting for her.

"I'm afraid you chose a bad night, Miss," he said.

She heard herself gasp, almost sob. "Oh, *no*."

"There's trouble over the Tamar Bridge," the man said. "Bomb scare. I've never known the like. Bloody vandals!"

"You mean the sleeper isn't going?" Ruth asked, beyond caring about reasons.

"It's going all right. But you'll have to get out at Saltash and go by coach over the road bridge. Then you'll be put on another sleeper at Plymouth station. So we're telling all the passengers in case they decide not to travel tonight."

"Oh, that's all right," she said, her voice trembling with relief. "I mean it could be a lot worse," she added, just wanting to get away and out of sight of anyone coming in to the station.

Her way was blocked by the porter.

"Mebyon Kernow, if you ask me," he said.

"Never," his colleague told him. "They're not like that."

"Well, is it likely to be bloody IRA? Or Scots Nats? Down here – they'd be a bit off beam, wouldn't they?"

"It's a hoax if you ask me. Students like as not. But you know the police, won't take any risks. Bloody students, excuse my French, Miss."

"Yes," she said, "well, I'm sure it will be all right – I must –"

"You're safe with us, Miss," he assured her.

"I hope you're right," she replied devoutly as she pushed her way past him.

She crossed the bridge just as the sleeper train was coming in.

"You've been told about the Saltash diversion?" the attendant asked, as she stood outside the door of her berth.

"Yes, thank you," she said, wanting nothing except to get inside and be safe, fearing that even at this late hour, Eliot might materialise at the end of the corridor.

"Good, I just wanted to tell you that it's not worth getting into bed," he explained with some embarrassment. "Not until you get on the next train at Plymouth. Then you can settle for the night."

"I quite understand."

The attendant was small, but persistent.

"By all means lie on your bunk, of course," he went on. "And don't worry about dropping off to sleep. We'll give you a call at Saltash."

"Thank you," she said.

He went at last. She could hear him beginning to explain to the next traveller as she opened her door. Then she was safely inside and had locked the door behind her. The window was closed – not that anyone could get in that tiny rectangle. She was safe in the solitude of her sleeper, as Michelle was safe in the community of her hospital ward.

She sat on the edge of her bunk, seized by a curious kind of numb exhaustion. The crazy shifts and dangers of the past few hours had tossed her about and left her here. Few hours? She looked at her watch. Five hours ago precisely she had been drinking in the pub bar with Eliot.

Eliot: the reversal of her feeling for him shocked her. Where there had been unquestioning trust there was now unreasoning terror. But real feelings don't change like that. It hadn't been real; it had all been nothing but fantasy and it had turned itself inside out as fantasies do. But the love and the fear both sprang from a sense of his total and unscrupulous power. And that had not changed.

It was all so much worse now that she had time to think.

The thoughts came crowding in. She shuddered convulsively as she remembered the dead weight of Michelle's body. She really had thought that she was dead. She had shut the thought out, but that was what she had believed until the moment of the nurse's pronouncement. The smell of gas filled her nostrils again and nauseated her. She leant over the basin but was not sick. She caught a glimpse of a drawn, pale face in the glass and almost screamed, not realising that it was her own. What a state of shattered nerves I am in, she thought, staring back at her reflection.

She must plan what to do. Since Michelle could not now go to London to the address she had been given, she must go in her place. She reached for her bag and made sure that she had her diary. It was there; the address was not far from Piccadilly. She would arrive too early to go straight there. She would wash and breakfast at Paddington and then go. She would be safe among the London crowds.

The train moved out of the station; it settled to a steady, rocking rhythm. She collapsed on her bunk like an exhausted animal.

CHAPTER FOURTEEN

Alastair stared out of the train window; drops of rain against black glass was all that he could see; a background for his own dimly reflected face. He looked at himself disapprovingly.

He despised himself in a way for making this journey. Yet part of him thought that it was a reasonable hope; surely the Ruth who had bought that ticket with him still existed somewhere. Although she had said she wouldn't come, although she had sent him her apologies for changing her mind, although she had sent him a cheque for the ticket with her thanks, surely there might still be, behind the sender of these painful courtesies, the shadow of a girl who had once nearly loved him and who might possibly find herself surprised into being pleased at seeing him again?

After all, she'd written before, hadn't she, telling him not to come to see her, then changed her mind and when she'd met him at the station had been so pleased to see him and they'd had some wonderful hours together, at first anyway. It wouldn't have happened if he'd just accepted her initial rejection, hadn't persisted.

He imagined going tomorrow into her attic room with its popping gas fire and its rickety table piled with books and papers, Ruth sitting at it, Ruth peering up at him short-sightedly as he stood in the doorway. And in that moment of surprise at seeing him – how would she look? He couldn't bear to think it might be an exasperated look, or worse still a polite attempt to hide the irritation which the very sight of him caused when she was hoping for, say, Eliot.

But it might not be like that: when she looked up, surprise might be replaced by joy as she rushed into his arms. It was worth trying. On the other hand, of course, she might still come to London, so he hadn't cancelled the room he'd booked for her in Mrs Goody's bed-and-breakfast establishment near to the boys' home though he'd warned her that his friend might not be able to come due to work.

"That's no problem," she'd told him. "It's a quiet time of year and I'll be sure to have a room to spare." Then she added, "I hope for your sake that the young lady will be able to come," and she'd looked sympathetically at him as if she understood the situation very well.

She was a kind person, he thought now. He'd got to know her when sometimes the boys' parents stayed with her; friendly and discreet, the warden called her. The warden had, unsolicited, given him a few days off. It seemed a good omen. Thoughts of Mrs Goody and Ruth and the warden swam about in his tired mind as he drifted off to sleep.

"Sorry, Sir," the guard repeated, "but it's all change at Plymouth."

"Oh, thank you."

He reached for his rucksack.

"Not yet, Sir. Twenty minutes to go. We're running late."

"But it's a through train," the woman in the opposite corner objected. "We never change at Plymouth."

Alastair looked at her, a determined-looking woman, youngish, bossy-voiced.

"And we're very late already," she accused.

"There's been a spot of bother, Ma'am," the guard explained with weary patience. He had been the length of the train explaining, always meeting the same objections. "Vandals messing about on the bridge. We'll be taking you round by coach. Then I'm afraid you'll have to wait at Saltash until we bring a train to take you down to Penzance."

He went on his way, apologising.

"It's ridiculous," the woman said to Alastair. "A put up job, if you ask me. They've been trying to close our line for years. My husband says the bridge won't survive another twenty years anyway and they'll never spend money replacing it, not with the railways losing money the way they do."

He wasn't really listening. He was thinking that he wouldn't mind being cut off with Ruth on the other side of the Tamar, but it would be unbearable if he was on one side of the river and she was on the other.

"Your husband works for the railways?" he asked, feigning polite interest. "That's how he knows?"

"Good gracious, no," she said, with a derisory laugh. "He's a stockbroker."

He nodded and settled himself to staring out of the window again.

"And I am on the Council," she said.

"Cornwall County Council?"

"No," she said. "Little Pentrenwatith."

There was silence between them as the train rattled along through the night. Somehow the threat to the bridge made him take rather less for granted the secure and easy rhythm of the train.

"It's in connection with my council work that I've been up to London," she said.

"Yes?"

"I've been buying an outfit for the Mayor's Foot Trundling."

"Oh?"

"There's so little choice in Cornwall," she explained, "and one has to have something suitable to the occasion."

"The occasion?"

"The trundling."

"Ah, yes, of course."

"We like to do what e can to maintain these old customs. They are part of a way of life which is fast disappearing."

"Yes, I suppose so. Television and so on."

"Even in the ten years *we've* lived down here things have declined. You'd hardly believe it."

"Oh, you're not Cornish?"

"Goodness, no. But it behoves people like us to show an example."

The train drew into the station. He lifted down her small case and large carrier bag, then, heaving his rucksack up on to his back, said good-night. As he turned, the rucksack caught her hat, tipping it forward over her face, but he did not hear her muffled protest and jumped down on to the platform.

The coach was waiting. As it drove them over the bridge, he looked at the rail bridge, sinuous and strong. It would be awful if anything happened to the Brunel bridge, he thought. He had been born in Devon; that bridge was part of his boyhood.

"In my opinion," the councillor was saying behind him. "It's the shape of things to come. I shall try to get a petition up. The trouble is, you know, between you and me, that country people are so apathetic."

Supposing, he thought again, just supposing she'd changed her mind and caught the sleeper after all? She was always impulsive. She probably hadn't got round to cashing the ticket in.

Supposing she had thought she would use it and surprise him. He despised himself again, as a nurturer of forlorn hopes and lost causes. But if she did, then they might cross each other on the way. It was perfectly possible. After all, she had no idea that he was coming. It was an absurd possibility that might wreck his life.

He had tried to ring her, after getting her letter. He had rung several times, he had even rung from the station before catching the train. But the bell must have rung out into an empty school. Unless of course she was alone there; up there in her room she wouldn't hear anything. He would ring her again from Saltash.

But at Saltash he had a better idea. He would ring Truro station and see if she had got on the sleeper. He collected plenty of small change and made for the telephone.

Of course, he thought as he rang the number, there'll be nobody there. There had been nobody on duty at the station when he had caught the sleeper that night. They collect the tickets on the train later.

But the telephone was picked up almost immediately.

"Is it possible," he asked, "to know if a passenger has caught the sleeper?"

"Any particular?" a slow voice asked.

"Well, yes, I did mean a particular one. A Miss Cassell. I wondered if you had a system of crossing the names off or something."

"No. No, there isn't no system as I know of."

"So you don't know if a Miss Cassell caught the sleeper? She had booked in advance."

There was a long and agonising pause.

"Couldn't say, Sir."

"I see. Thank you. I'm sorry to have troubled you."

Perhaps the wires caught something of the despair he felt and carried it to the listening ear. He was just going to put the receiver down when he heard the voice at the other end say, "Tonight of course we did stop everybody because of the bridge like."

"You did? Then –"

"We had to tell them, you see; I mean in case they didn't want to travel in the circumstances."

"Do you remember if you saw a girl with fair hair? She might have been wearing glasses. She might have been wearing a blue coat, or –"

"I didn't check the passengers myself."

"Would it be possible to ask? I mean is there somebody there? It's rather important. I mean I need to know where she is –"

All the world loves a lover. "I'll get my colleague," the man said and put the receiver down with a clatter.

Alastair waited, feeding coins into the slot every few seconds.

"Good evening, Sir. Can I help you?"

The voice was brisk, business-like.

He explained.

"Well now," it replied, this voice which, in his overwrought state, he thought could make or mar his life. "There were five passengers got on. There were two gents together and a couple and a single lady. Whether it was your young lady, I can't say."

"I see. Well. Thank you."

Oh God, it only made it worse. There was now a chance that she was on the train. If he caught his connection to Truro from here in a few minutes, he might pass her in the night.

"But I could go and look on the list and see how many single ladies there were intending to join the train at Truro."

"Oh yes, please."

Another long pause; he fed more coins into the hungry slot.

"It must have been your lady, Sir. There aren't any others on the list getting on here. Just a Miss Cassell, first class. There was a gent who didn't turn up, but it was a company booking and they often change their minds. You know how it is."

Alastair didn't know how it was, he didn't care how it was. He just knew that she was coming.

"You're sure? Nobody else could have got on – I mean if it wasn't her?"

"Impossible Sir, We'd have to ring Penzance for the booking. The only booking we have is this Miss Cassell."

"Thank you, thank you very much."

"Pleasure Sir. Glad to oblige."

"Oh just one more thing?"

"Yes Sir?" the voice asked warily, a shade less than glad.

"Did it leave on time?"

"It left here on time. There's no trouble down this end, you know. It's they Devon folk that's doing it."

"Thank you again. Oh, thank you very much."

He liked this man, he would happily have spent the rest of the time, until she came, chatting to him. But the line had gone dead.

As he came out of the telephone box, his fellow passengers were being summoned on to the platform. "The special train to Truro is just coming in, Sir," the guard said to him. "A couple of minutes. Sorry you've had this delay, but we can't take any risks. It doesn't do to ignore warnings."

"Oh, that's all right." He was grinning all over his face. "I'm not going."

"Not going on? After waiting all this time?"

"No, I'm meeting the sleeper from Truro. Which platform will it arrive at?"

"The sleeper, Sir? Over the bridge, platform six."

"It's coming at last," the Councillor remarked, as he passed her.

"I'm not coming," he called back, as he made for the bridge.

"Extraordinary," he heard the clear, bossy voice say. "I can't make these young people out nowadays. So unreliable."

He heard her train coming in as he crossed the bridge. On platform six he settled himself down on a bench to await the sleeper.

CHAPTER FIFTEEN

She must have dozed. She had wild dreams. She was being hunted by the police. They accused her of murder. They said she had killed her father, but it wasn't true. Tears ran down her face at the thought of it. She tried to explain but they locked her in a cell. They beat on the walls of the cell to torment her. She was not allowed to sleep. She longed for sleep but they woke her with their knocking.

She woke with a start; it wasn't a dream, somebody was really knocking. A man's voice was saying something about tea or coffee. She couldn't make it out, for the train was crashing noisily through a tunnel. She said, "Tea, please," but he went on saying something, his accent very Cornish. They must be coming into Saltash, she supposed. She got up and stumbled over to the door and unlocked it.

Immediately the door opened and an arm appeared holding a blue grip which jammed the door open. She fell back as a man followed the grip into the compartment and banged the door closed behind him, leant against it, glaring at her. It was Eliot. It was all done before she had time to realise what was happening.

"Thank you, my dear," Eliot drawled, leaning back against the door. "Thank you very much for being so hospitable."

His face was venomous. His glaring eyes were bloodshot. He had been drinking: the smell of it filled the tiny compartment. She couldn't speak, only stare in horror.

The train emerged from the tunnel. It was suddenly quiet.

"If you scream," he said. "'I'll strangle you now."

The implication that is she didn't scream he would strangle her later, did not escape her.

"So," he went on, "you thought you'd slip away, did you? You little bitch! You've been play-acting all these weeks, leading me on and then –"

"Eliot, it wasn't like that," she said, but stopped, hating herself for pleading.

"What was it like then? When did you change your mind? I'm going to get the truth out of you before I shut you up for good."

"I did mean to stay with you. Really I did. It was only when I heard the telephone call and realised that you were in with them – with those two –"

"So that was it. Well, well."

Sometime between here and Saltash he would do it. She must try to keep him talking; it was her only hope.

"If you'd just dashed away on an impulse," Eliot was saying, "I'd have understood that, but you plotted and schemed, didn't you? 'Let's have a bath, dear Eliot,' – you bitch. You were laughing at me all the time. That was your mistake. I don't like being laughed at, never have. I don't forgive it."

He moved suddenly and she prepared to struggle, but he only bent down and took a bottle of whisky out of the grip.

"Hand me that glass," he ordered.

She handed it to him. He filled it and drank.

He is getting his courage up to kill me, she thought.

"You took me on a bit of a wild goose chase," he remarked. "You've had me running round town in Bill's car half the night. I'd like to know where you were."

She didn't answer. She tried to think quickly; it would be better not to tell him about Michelle. Anything that she knew that he did not, must surely add to her strength.

"Why didn't you catch the earlier train?" he asked suddenly. "You had plenty of time."

"I had the sleeper reservation," she said. "Alastair got it for me that weekend."

"Oh," he said smiling malignantly. "Young Lochinvar, eh?" Slowly he took a wallet out of his pocket: Alastair's wallet.

She almost screamed, imagining for an appalled moment that he must have killed Alastair to get it. In his murderer's hands it seemed it must be the possession of the dead.

"So it was *you* who stole it."

"Yes, I must say I enjoyed that meal – paid for by the dear, unwitting Alastair."

"But why? What did Alastair and I matter to you?"

"Because by that time, my brief was to distract the attention of the pretty new History mistress, friend of Michelle."

His voice was bitter. "I had failed in my main task. I always do. You see before you a picture of failure; it's safe to tell you because you won't be able to tell anybody else."

He was going to confess to her; that was a bad sign.

The train rattled gently through the night; otherwise it was quiet except for the noise of Eliot's swallowing whisky. If she screamed would anyone hear? Eliot was sitting with his back against the door, knees wide apart, his hands dangling between them. The replenished tumbler was on the floor beside him.

"But it wasn't my fault," he said petulantly. "How should I know you'd change clothes? *Women!* I thought it was her until I heard your well-bred little English voice call out."

"It was you?" she whispered in horror. "You in the drive that night?"

"Who else?" he asked, tossing back another whisky.

"I thought it was Albert," she blurted out.

"Albert?"

He put down the empty glass, threw back his head and laughed. She could see right down into his mouth: big teeth, lolling furred tongue. What strange lycanthropy had transformed her gentle Eliot into this wolf-creature?

"Albert, my God, that's rich! Tell me why you thought it was Albert?"

When she did not reply, he began to get up and she knew that if she crossed him he would kill her now. She must keep talking: it was her only chance.

"Because he didn't run after me. I knew it was somebody strong, but he didn't run after me. So I thought it was Albert."

"Albert! I can't get over it. That gentle old fool Albert! Do you know something? The cat brought a mouse into his room a bit ago and what does the old fool do? Rescues the mouse – gets scratched for his pains and serve him right. Then he nurses it in his room in a little box full of straw and when it's better, sets it free. Ye gods, Albert a murderer!"

He took the bottle again. "I'll drink to that," he said and this time he drank straight from the whisky bottle. "What would Albert want a girl for anyway? He hasn't been much good to the ladies for many a year. Poor old Albert, well, well."

Even now, she thought, the gas is flowing through Michelle's open door and along the corridors. It is seeping into Albert's room where he lies on the sacks. I should have turned it off. Through my negligence I have murdered a good old man.

"No," Eliot was saying, "the idea in the woods was not sex but murder, straightforward murder. But speaking of such things, my dear, there's time for both tonight."

He filled the glass and raised it ceremoniously.

"Here's to your very good health," he mocked. "Yes, I had high hopes tonight, but it's all coming right in the end. We can share that bunk, my dear, before we part company for good. I shall have – how shall I put it? A free ride. The night is yet young. Plenty of time before we get to Paddington. I should say before *you* get to Paddington. I shall probably leave you at Reading."

He didn't know, he didn't know, he didn't know about the bridge. They hadn't told him.

She covered her face with her hands so that he shouldn't see the relief. But she must know for sure.

"How did you get on the train?" she asked, as casually as she could.

"By the back door," he said. "I've plenty of practice in getting on trains without paying; it came in useful tonight. Nobody knows that I'm on this train except you and me. And when I leave you I shall get off by the back door too. And then nobody will know that I have been here, except myself."

"You don't propose to throw my body out of the window then?"

"Impossible. You're a big girl now. Besides there's no need. They'll find you here. On your bunk. Modestly covered with your blanket, I promise."

He got up. She must keep him talking until Saltash.

"One thing I don't understand," she said.

"Yes?" He hesitated, enjoying power too much to rush to its conclusion. Then he sat down again and filled his glass.

"How did you know I was on the sleeper? I might have gone on an earlier train or stayed in Truro or anything?"

"Ah," he said, obviously pleased with himself. "You're not much of a schemer, are you? At six o'clock every night they put up a list at Truro Station of the names of passengers travelling on the sleeper. It even gives the number and class of the berth. Little girls who are running away secretly, shouldn't use the sleeper."

"And what did you do then?"

"All I had to do was make a note of which berth you were in, go away and fill in time having a drink or two and stock up with a bottle for the journey, then I went back to the station and slipped on to the train while you were chatting to the attendant. I waited a bit in the lavatory until we reached the tunnel, which seemed a good time to drop in and see you."

She made herself speak calmly. "But just because your pride is hurt because I didn't spend the weekend with you, it's a bit drastic to kill me, isn't it? I mean you can get into real trouble for doing that, you know. It's a hanging offence."

"I can't risk leaving you free, you must see that," he apologised, shaking his head. "Nobody regrets it more than I do. After all we've had some good times together, haven't we?"

He was mad. She couldn't bear to look at him; this caricature of the face of the man she had loved and trusted.

"When Michelle is found dead, you'll move heaven and earth to know the reason why. Or you would, if I let you go."

The words hung in the air between them, menacing her. She talked quickly to dispel them.

"No, I won't Eliot, I promise."

"I'd like to oblige you, my dear," he said, "but I can't risk it. Besides my task was to keep you out of the way: I've failed in my first approach, but there are more ways than one of keeping you out of the way."

He held out his hands significantly. They were dirty.

"Besides, how could I go back and tell them I've failed again?" Petulance was edging its way into his voice. "What do you think it was like having to admit I'd failed last time? This time they've taken over the important part."

"They?"

"Yes, *they*. Oh, I know Mrs Sweetness-and-Light Bland takes you in like everybody else, but she's in it every bit as much as Esther Fairbairn."

She did not want to hear. Even now, when her own danger would have blotted out everything else, she didn't want to hear evil of Eleanor Bland.

"I suppose," she said conversationally, "it is always hard to think of one's employer as a murderess. It somehow doesn't fit the Headmistress image either."

"You're cool," Eliot said. "I like that." He imitated her voice. "Let us discuss the position of the murderess in society, vis à vis that of the Headmistress."

He giggled and drank again.

She laughed and said lightly, "Now there's a subject for a thesis–"

He turned on her. "It is no laughing matter what that bloody Bland woman has done to Esther. I'll tell you about Eleanor Bland. She's the sort who wants all the profits and none of the dirty work. She knew damn well when they decided to ask Michelle over here what Esther would have to do, but she shut her eyes to it. 'We're having my heiress niece over, Eliot, just to keep an eye on her', she'd say in that silly mincing little voice. 'So kind of dear Esther,' but she knew all right. Dear Esther could do the dirty work and Eleanor would know absolutely nothing – officially. I've warned Esther. In a court of law, I told her, Eleanor Bland would swear she had no idea what was going on."

"And what did Esther say?"

"She said she had no intention of letting either of them appear in a court of law. Eleanor was not to be sullied with sordid details about murder. Her mind was on higher things."

"But Esther doesn't even like the school."

"You can say that again. The unwritten ladies' agreement was that if anything should happen to poor dear Michelle, so that the land was Eleanor's, then it would be sold for development for a quarter of a million and they'd live happily ever after. I'd have my cut, of course, for services rendered. And the two of them would retire to a love nest; that's how Esther saw it. But I wonder. I wouldn't put it past Eleanor Bland to ditch Esther once she'd played her part. Maybe she meant it at the beginning, but she's grown obsessed with that school. Build it up, get more staff. What the hell did she want to go appointing you for? They could have got on. The school only had to tick over, it was only a blind, but I've watched Eleanor Bland these last few years and the school was mattering more and more. I think Esther suspected it too, but she's besotted."

He stretched and took another drink. "We shall see," he said. "I shall have a talk with Esther when I get back – and I shall go back as soon as possible. I'm taking risks coming up country with you like this, you know. I'm on the run. I'm supposed to be keeping nicely hidden in Cornwall until a certain little matter of forgery has blown over. I'll settle this business and back I'll go."

"By 'this business' you mean my untimely death?"

"And Michelle's. I'll tell you about her, shall I?" he hesitated. "No harm now. She's dead by now, your poor friend, the little French stumbling block. And dead before her twenty-first birthday too, which makes things simpler, and incidentally saves death duties."

"You think you'll get away with it?"

"Foolproof – better than the rapist in the woods. You can't do that twice anyway. I'll tell you about the death of your friend: poor little soul was so lonely left up there when everybody else was on holiday that she took her life by gas poisoning. Sad, but understandable. Tragic for the Head and Housekeeper, who will of course blame themselves for leaving her alone, but she had insisted – despite all sorts of kind invitations – upon staying. It must have been an impulse, what could be more natural than to commit suicide when you are a lonely stranger in a foreign land?"

"Except that suicides don't block the door with rolls of carpet on the outside first."

"That will be removed on Monday by my dear thoughtful sister before she raises the alarm."

He put down his glass.

"How did you know about that?" he asked. Then, suddenly understanding, he added, "So you went there. That's where you were."

"Eliot," she said urgently. "She isn't dead. She's recovering in hospital. No murder has been committed. The hospital think it's suicide. You can all get off. Michelle can easily say it was a silly accident or the fire blew out. I'll back the story up. You need not been involved. Just get off the train at the next stop. I'll give you my ticket."

He stared at her thoughtfully. He was weighing up her life. "No," he said. "*You* know. Michelle may be persuaded she did it herself. But *you* saw the carpet rolled up on the outside of the door. *You* know."

Too late she realised that she had signed her own death warrant.

"Eliot," she said, "before you do anything, there are things I want to know. Just tell me. I have a right to know –"

He watched, smiling. It pleased his vanity to be appealed to. He was torn between the need to act and the claims of vanity.

"When you said your sister –"

"Esther's my sister, God help me. If only she hadn't been, it would all have been different."

He groaned and put his head into his hands.

"She was always better at everything. They used to try to make out that she wasn't, that I had all the real talent – it was well hidden, they said, I was just a bit lazy, they said, I was a late developer, they said. I liked to hear it, that I was the brilliant one and she was just a plodder. She did stick at things, it was true, but she was clever too. I knew it really, but I let them spoil me. I let them wreck her life. I should have stood up for her."

He looked up and she saw that the bloodshot eyes were filled with tears.

"If she'd been weaker, if she'd been just a little bit dependent on me, I would have helped her, supported her, anything. But she was tough. Tougher than me. She bore everything, never complained, accepted their verdict, but she knew. She knew me too, knew me through and through. She read her big brother like a book."

He took another long drink from the bottle.

"If I'd been the younger one it wouldn't have been so bad; I'd just have let her be boss, and worship her. But I couldn't; I had to pretend to be tougher and cleverer just because I was older. I bluffed from childhood – I've had to bluff. I can't help myself now –"

"But you can. Eliot, believe me, not just for my sake. For yours too. You can break free don't just blame circumstances–"

He smiled mournfully. "The fault, dear Brutus, is not in our stars, but in ourselves," he quoted lugubriously. "Oh, yes, I know a lot of that stuff. Nearly went on the stage, you know; spent all my time at University acting instead of getting on with my work. If I hadn't been so talented, I might have got a degree."

"Poor Eliot," she said.

He turned on her.

"I can do without your pity," he snarled. Then his face softened and his voice was gentle, almost caressing, as he said, "Oh Ruth, Ruth, why wouldn't you be warned? I tried to warn you. I didn't want to hurt you. I told you I was a wastrel, a no-good, a sponger."

"You told me about Esther's brother."

"But you didn't guess. I wanted you to guess."

He began to rock himself to and fro, as he sat there on his haunches, hand swinging between his knees.

"I tried to get rid of you. It was all your fault."

"*My* fault?"

"Yes, yours. Oh God, you women. There you were demanding to be loved and cherished and fathered. Why couldn't you have stuck to young Lochinvar? But you had to tempt me, didn't you? You had to make me play the role of the dependable older man, so that you could feel safe."

She stared at him; it was true. She had made herself his victim.

The train was slowing down.

"Must be coming to the bridge," he remarked, his voice suddenly practical. "Plymouth soon."

"Oh well," she said. "At least I shall be spared to see the bridge again. I loved watching the road bridge from the train when I came."

"You won't see it," he said. "It's on the other side. You're hopeless about things like that, aren't you?"

"No, it's on the right side. I remember when I came."

"You were coming the other way then. It's upstream, I tell you."

"Bet you five pounds we'll see it out of that window."

"My God, you're cool, aren't you?"

"Well if I'm to be raped and strangled, I might as well die a gambler too."

"I like you," he said quietly. Then the petulance returned. "Why have you made me kill you?"

The train was drawing to a standstill.

"What are we stopping here for?" he asked. "We don't stop at Saltash."

"Refuelling or something, I expect."

"That's aeroplanes," he said and laughed.

She was straining her ears to any sound from the corridor. She thought she could hear people moving. She talked rapidly to distract him.

"I don't think it's Saltash," she said. "We're not there yet. Let's look out and see."

"Not you. You stay where you are," he ordered, not taking his eyes off her as he got up and crossed the compartment.

"I'm not moving," she assured him. "I want to win my bet about the bridge."

He opened the little sliding window and peered out.

She flung herself at the door, scrabbling wildly at the handle. Eliot turned and snatched at her arm to pull her back. But as the train stopped with a tremendous jolt, the door flew back on its hinges and she fell out into the corridor. The little attendant who had been standing outside, his hand raised ready to knock at her door, staggered as she fell heavily against him and, together, they reeled back against the corridor window. Other passengers were standing waiting to get out. She saw their astonished faces as she clung to the attendant. But strangest of all, there on the platform was Alastair. She could see him through the window over the attendant's shoulder. With his rucksack on the bench beside him he was sitting there waiting for her, sound asleep.

CHAPTER SIXTEEN

The explosion at Polglaze School on Monday afternoon was headline news in the *West Briton*. Returning from a brief rest in the Scilly Isles the Headmistress and the Housekeeper could scarcely have been in the building for more than a few minutes when the whole place went up. Investigations revealed that a major gas escape had taken place which must eventually have filled the whole basement and found its way into the boiler room. The coke boiler, a gas board spokesman explained, worked by drawing in air. This time it had drawn in gas. The two women were on the ground floor and must have been killed immediately.

A young French girl, presumed to be an Assistante at the school, had a lucky escape. Being briefly in hospital at the time of the explosion, she was out of harm's way and was now being looked after by friends in London. Search was still going on, however, for the body of an elderly caretaker believed to have been in the basement when the explosion occurred. The work was necessarily slow, and heavy machinery was being used to clear the rubble.

The miracle was, the paper pointed out, that all the girls and the rest of the staff were away for half term. Had the explosion taken place in term time, the resultant tragedy did not bear contemplation.

Arrangements were being made for the children to complete the term in other schools and the Senior Mistress was in charge of all enquiries by parents.

Some of the national papers carried the story too. Later they all reported the true-life story of the caretaker saved by the cat. The cat it seemed had been affected by the fumes and had made its way to the caretaker's room where it had collapsed. Very early on Saturday morning, though feeling unwell himself, the caretaker had carried it down to the vet. Seeing that he was ill, the vet had taken the old man to stay with his nephew in a caravan outside the town. Therefore when the explosion occurred, both cat and caretaker were safely away from the school. Both were now doing well.

Sunday morning, bright and blustery. Leaves spiralling off the trees in the park, rustling under their feet.

"I can't believe," Ruth said, as they sat on the bench "that I really slept for twenty-four hours. I don't usually manage the statutory eight."

"You were exhausted."

"The last thing I remember is your Mrs Goody lending me her nightie early yesterday morning and tucking me up with a hot water bottle. And the next minute it was this morning and she was bringing in my breakfast. She's been wonderful, treated me like a cross between a Victorian invalid lady and a favourite niece."

Alastair smiled down at her.

"I didn't go into details but I did let her know you'd had a terrible, terrible time and needed cherishing."

"She's done more than just cherish me. Do you know, she whisked my clothes away, washed and ironed them and there they were, neatly folded on my chair this morning? And all the time I just slept."

"Well, she was a bit concerned that you hadn't any spare clothes with you."

"I've got plenty at home."

They were silent for a while, both realising how naturally, how easily she'd spoken the words, *At Home*. That meant at home with her father and Elizabeth, which was where they were going now. They'd taken the bus to the park so they could walk the rest of the way, give her time to adjust to the old surroundings, Alastair thought.

"It's going to be all right," he reassured her reading her thoughts.

"We're early," she said. "Let's sit for a while."

The bench caught the sun, the autumn sun, low in the sky. They sat, his arm around her, her head on his shoulder.

"Go on telling me about the Fourniers," she said.

"Well, I went to see them on Saturday morning –"

"Why weren't you exhausted?" she interrupted. "You'd been up all night too."

"I don't know. I was just bursting with energy. I couldn't rest. They were very welcoming. I mean they didn't know me, but they took me in and rang Monsieur Guyomarc'h, who is coming over tomorrow and once Michelle is fit he'll sort out the business of the land and school. Apparently her parents were very naive and never did anything about this inheritance."

"I think that's awful. They should have done something about it for Michelle's sake."

"Yes, but there were more urgent matters than worrying about a bit of property in Britain. And anyway it had been requisitioned by the government for a school evacuated from London. It must have been marvellous for the kids, escaping the blitz."

"But after the war?"

"Well, things were unsettled for years afterwards, bad enough in Britain but much worse in occupied Europe. And her parents were young, they probably thought there was plenty of time to sort it out. So it drifted, and Mrs Bland seized the opportunity. They think that at first she'd just hoped to buy it cheaply from her sister, telling her what a rundown old building it was, but later, after her sister and her husband had died, the three of them worked out this scheme that she'd inherit the place if Michelle was disposed of. Hence the invitation."

Ruth shivered.

"You're cold?"

"No, it's not that."

She buried her face in his shoulder and whispered, "I still can't believe that anyone could be so utterly wicked. I mean to be so calculating, just to get money. Eliot was mad, I'm sure of that now –"

She stopped. It was the first time she'd said his name since he was going to kill her in the sleeper. Just uttering those three little syllables brought it all back as she choked and shuddered and couldn't go on.

He held her close.

"It's all right, darling, it' s over. Let me tell you what we've arranged. The Fourniers have talked to the hospital and are driving down today to see how she is. If she's fit, they'll bring her back tomorrow. They have a room ready for her. You can see her any time."

He went on talking, soothing, giving her time to recover.

At last she stopped shaking and looked up at him.

"Poor Michelle," she said. "What a dreadful time she's had."

"Easier than yours," he told her. "She just went to sleep and woke up in hospital, feeling ghastly maybe, but she didn't have to go through what you did. And you saved her, Ruth, you saved her life. When you feel dreadful about it all, just remind yourself that you saved a friend's life. Not many people can say that."

"Well, you saved my sanity at Saltash. All those questions, I couldn't have got through it on my own. And then he was still there –"

"He was a fool, he might have got away with it if he'd slipped off quietly, but he ranted and raged and fought the man who asked for his ticket. And once the police were called and you told them he was Eliot Fairbairn, the man on the run for fraud charges, he was carted off. He was a fool to tell you that anyway."

"But you see he didn't think I'd live to tell anyone."

He cursed himself for what he'd said – of all the silly tactless things, reminding her of the scene in the sleeper.

"I'm sorry."

Her reply surprised him.

"Alastair," she said. "Do you remember when you came and I met you at the station and we walked to the bistro?"

"Yes, it's not the sort of thing I'd ever forget."

"And you asked me something?"

"And you said 'No'."

He was sitting up now, looking at her, suddenly alert.

"Afterwards I thought I should have said yes, but then it all unravelled somehow and I never did."

He took both her hands in his, held her a little away from him.

"And if I asked you again now, what would you say?"

It seemed to last a long time, that silence. They just looked at each other until at last she said very quietly, "I'd say yes."

Two children, passing by with their mother, looked with interest at this couple, wrapped round each other on the bench, not moving, evidently oblivious of the world around them. Fascinated, the children stood and stared. Then their mother pulled them away. A little later a dog came and snuffled them. "Down, Rover," a man called. "Come here. Heel, sir, heel."

And still they didn't move, until at last she looked up and smiled.

"Penny for them?" Alastair asked.

"I was remembering that I meant to tell you very privately over a glass of wine in a romantic restaurant with candles on the table. And actually I've done it in a very public place on a park bench with a litter bin stuck on its side."

"I don't care where it is, so long as you say it."

This required more kissing, then he added, "Would tomorrow be a good day to find you a ring? I've still got two days' leave."

"I've no other plans," she told him. "Apart from seeing a lot of Michelle."

"Yes, she'll need help, filling in time while she waits for Guyomarc'h to sort things out."

"Oh, she'll be busy. I can tell you exactly what she'll do. She'll buy yards of material and make lots of lovely clothes."

"Is she good at making wedding dresses?"

She laughed and hugged him, then added, "But seriously, it's going to be a long engagement, isn't it?"

"Yes, we've both to sort out what we're going to do. I shan't earn much for three years. And we'll have to save for a deposit on a house."

"And I'll have to find out about teacher training. I don't expect I can start until September."

He stood up, "Come on, time to move. Let's not worry about the future today. The present is good enough."

It wasn't far to the house. They walked in step, arms around each other out of the park into the familiar road and up the avenue to the house, as she had done so many times before. All those years, she had lived here, Professor Cassell's daughter. Until the day when he had said, "Ruth, this is Elizabeth," and everything had changed. So she was quiet as they walked.

"It's going to be all right," Alastair told her again. She rang the bell; she didn't have a key now.

It was Elizabeth who opened the door, her father standing just behind her. Both had their arms open in welcome.

"Elizabeth," Ruth said, as they went indoors. "This is Alastair."

Printed in Poland
by Amazon Fulfillment
Poland Sp. z o.o., Wrocław

54022288R00065